DAPHNE CLAIR

a ruling passion

Harlequin Books

TORONTO • NEW YORK • LONDON
AMSTERDAM • PARIS • SYDNEY • HAMBURG
STOCKHOLM • ATHENS • TOKYO • MILAN

Harlequin Presents first edition April 1984
ISBN 0-373-10679-3

Original hardcover edition published in 1983
by Mills & Boon Limited

CHAPTER ONE

THEY said it always rained in Westland. Not true, Richard Lewis knew. For five days he had enjoyed glorious weather—brilliant sunshine and clear skies, 'The Coast' belying its reputation. But now on Saturday the rain had come, persistent and with a chill in it. He had put on a suit and tie, and tossed a gaberdine raincoat on the back seat of the Mercedes this morning before starting the trip from Hokitika. He would have preferred slacks and a casual jacket, but knew that a suit created an instant impression when he was making business calls.

He slowed the car, peering at a black-on-yellow AA sign that pointed down a side road leading inland, away from the silvery, windtossed waters of the Tasman that washed the long coastline. The rain obscured his vision, and he braked, winding down the window to lean out and see the printed lettering.

The name of the road matched the scribbled note that lay on the dashboard shelf in front of him. Closing the window, he brushed raindrops impatiently from his face and his dark russet hair, and turned the car down the narrow road.

It was unsealed, and he cursed quietly as the Mercedes bounced into a series of potholes, making the steering wheel spin in his hands until his tightened grip forced it to steady up. The windscreen wipers slicked back and forth, and something loomed in front through the misty rain, then roared past in a blur, spraying up a fountain of reddish mud that for a few moments covered the windscreen and stopped him from seeing anything.

He slammed on the brakes until the wipers cleared their two arcs, then went forward again. No other vehicles came at him, but the rain was falling in a steady stream, and he was careful now to slow whenever a suspiciously rough-looking piece of road showed up. He had been told that Alex Cameron's studio was about seven miles along this road, only a couple of miles before it ended at the re-opened goldmine which was slated to become a major tourist attraction. Personally, he thought that unless the road was upgraded the tourists were likely to stay away from the place in their thousands.

He was travelling very slowly; maybe that was why the distance seemed so long. Also, he had found, West Coasters not only managed to largely ignore the kilometric system to which the whole of New Zealand was supposed to have converted years ago, they also had a very elastic idea of the length of a mile. In only five days he had learned to add a mile or two to any estimate of distance. Today he was not in a tolerant mood. Besides the weather, he had already had to cope that morning with a flustered waitress at breakfast who had muddled the orders and brought him sausages, which he hated, instead of bacon and eggs; a punctured tyre that had forced him to pull into a garage which was fortuitously handy, but whose proprietor had treated him to a display of veiled sarcasm designed to emphasise how 'city' (he made it sound suspiciously like 'sissy') gentlemen who couldn't or wouldn't change their own tyres were of a species not quite on a level with real men; and a missed turning owing to some vandals having removed a signpost.

When he saw a large and colourful sign ahead, he assumed he had reached his destination, only to blink in disbelief and give vent to an irritated expletive when he saw that it was fixed to the gateway of the goldmine it advertised. He had come too far. Obviously he had somehow missed Alex Cameron's studio.

There was no place to turn the car, except inside the gateway, so he crossed the cattle-stop at the entrance and drove into the small car-park. The rain had lifted temporarily, and from a small, restored nineteenth-century cottage, a bearded, fair-haired young giant emerged, dressed in a denim shirt with rolled shirtsleeves, faded trews and long boots. A floppy felt hat completed the illusion of an apparition from the past.

He was heading purposefully for the car, and from common courtesy Richard was compelled to brake, wind down the window, and wait.

The giant bent to peer in at him, a genial smile bisecting the beard. 'Come to see the mine?' he enquired hopefully.

'I'm afraid not—I missed my way. I hope you don't mind my using your car-park to turn.'

'Help yourself. Where were you heading?'

'Alex Cameron's studio. I was told it's on this road.'

If anything, the grin became even wider. 'Alex's? You missed it, all right! Go back down the road about two miles. Watch for a couple of big trees at the gateway, on your left. You can't miss it.'

Quelling an impulse to retort that he had

already done so once, after being told yesterday that he couldn't, Richard said, 'Thanks,' and put the car into reverse. The giant watched him complete the turn, gave him a friendly wave and went back into the house.

The rain came down again, and if it hadn't been for the landmark of the two big trees, as mentioned, he might have passed the place again. There was a sign, but it was modest compared with the goldmine's self-advertisement, just a stained timber board with white lettering swinging beside the gate, proclaiming, ALEX CAMERON: THE STUDIO. And the trees overhung it, so that it was difficult to see from the road unless one was looking carefully. Irritation rose again. Surely if the man wanted business he should ensure that those who wanted to buy his work could find him!

There was a depression in the drive right in the gateway, and the tyres splashed through it, spraying more muddy water over the paintwork. He resigned himself to having to clean the car when he returned to his hotel. Presumably there would be some sort of car-wash arrangement.

The drive wound around between trees and stopped abruptly in front of an old house of similar vintage to the one at the mine. This one needed painting, but otherwise seemed to be in good repair. There was a covered veranda in front of which he parked the car in a cleared space seemingly designed for visitors' vehicles. To one side a small garage with its door open housed a shabby Volkswagen Beetle.

He didn't identify the sound he heard as he got out of the car and carefully stepped over a large and very dirty puddle, until the horse rounded the corner of the house and its rider uttered a surprised 'Whoa!' and pulled it up short, snorting. Its flurrying hooves in the soft, wet ground created little plopping spurts of mud.

It was still a few feet away, but Richard was startled and stepped backwards into the puddle. The water covered one shoe and he felt his heel sinking into oozing slime before he pulled it free and surveyed his trousers, mud-speckled almost to the knees, and with the edges soaked.

He bent to ruefully wring out some of the excess water, and the child who had been riding the horse bareback slid off, leading the animal towards him. 'I'm sorry! Did I scàre you?'

A boy of about ten or so, Richard guessed, looking up. Dressed in jeans and a shabby tee-shirt, inadequately protected from the rain by a short yellow nylon jacket, with the front unfastened, and the hood pushed back from fair, tousled, straight hair. The green eyes were anxiously apologetic. A nice-looking kid, with a healthy suntan and a peppering of freckles across his nose.

Suppressing a natural temptation to snap, Richard straightened, saying rather shortly, 'No. I just wasn't expecting a horse to come round the corner so suddenly. My fault, no doubt.'

Missing the irony in his tone, the child grinned widely, saying in a relieved voice, 'Oh, that's all right, then. Hey, that's a Mercedes, isn't it?'

He came closer to inspect the car, and the horse perforce followed. It was a very large horse, with a long, ugly, fiddle-shaped head, particularly knobbly knees, and a bony-looking back that looked as though it could have carried an entire family of seven or so. It seemed very big for the boy.

It apparently had a friendly nature, however, for it turned its head curiously towards Richard and nuzzled in a confiding manner at his shoulder, blowing a long streak of horsy saliva down his jacket.

'Yes, it is,' Richard said, repelling these unwelcome advances.

'Can I touch it?'

'Be my guest. You can sit in it, if you like, but I'm afraid there isn't room for the horse.'

The boy chuckled. 'I'll put him away in the paddock. Come on, Casanova.'

'Casanova?' Richard murmured, casting a dubious eye over the animal's unlovely lines.

The boy laughed again. 'Mum named him. He's a gelding, really. It's a joke.'

Gathering up the reins, he gave the horse a shove, and Casanova obligingly backed away.

Richard said, 'Just a minute, son. Is your father about?'

He didn't know why that should produce a gale of laughter, but while he waited politely for it to abate he took his handkerchief from his breast pocket and shook out the folds to wipe off Casanova's greeting.

'I'm not a "son", actually,' the child said. 'My name's Jane.'

Richard said resignedly, 'I beg your pardon, Jane. I didn't mean to be rude, but it's hard to tell these days. Everyone wears jeans and tee-shirts, and the same kinds of haircuts.'

'Oh, that's all right,' Jane said handsomely. 'I don't think it's rude to make a mistake.'

Rubbing at his shoulder with the handkerchief, Richard didn't notice the woman who had appeared on the veranda from the house until

Jane said, 'Hey, Mum, we've got a visitor. He said I can have a look inside his car, when I've got rid of Cas.'

As Jane led the horse away the woman said, 'That's nice of him.'

He looked up, his handkerchief still bundled in his hand, attracted by the slightly husky, warm tone of her voice.

She was very like her daughter, with the same clear jade eyes and honey blonde hair, hers cut to swing about her shoulders, gently curving under. The freckles were missing, but the nose was an adult and unfreckled version of Jane's, straight but with an unexpected width at the nostrils hinting at a less cool nature than the green eyes betrayed. And her mouth, although unpainted, was decidedly feminine, as was the shape of her body. She wore a tee-shirt, too, black and scooped at the neckline, clinging to rounded breasts and a slender midriff. He would have taken a bet she was wearing no bra. A long skirt printed with a striking pattern in black, brown and white was tied about her waist and, as it just cleared the worn boards of the veranda, he could see that she was not only bra-less but shoeless as well.

It hadn't taken him a second to make the quick appraisal, but as his eyes returned to hers, he saw that he in turn was being subjected to a fairly thorough scrutiny. She surveyed him quite slowly from Casanova's mark still faintly showing on his shoulder to the mud clinging to his trousers and seeping from his soaked pigskin shoes, then let her gaze linger momentarily on the buttoned waistcoat and the dark silk tie. When her eyes finally returned to his he found himself profoundly irritated again, because he discerned in their limpid depths an unmistakable gleam of amusement. He wasn't a vain man, but he had long since become aware that most women on first acquaintance regarded him with some interest. They didn't usually react to meeting him with an ill-concealed desire to laugh.

He stuffed the handkerchief into his hip pocket with an impatient hand and went up the two steps on to the veranda. At least it put him on a level with her, and more. Even without the advantage of the differing heights between veranda and ground, she was a tall woman, probably about five feet eight or nine in those bare feet, but he was still half a head taller.

Smoothly he said, 'Good morning, Mrs Cameron. I wondered if I might see some of your husband's work. And I'd like very much to meet him, if he's about?'

The laughter in her eyes became more pronounced, and her smile had a mocking twist to it, as her eyebrows arched delicately. 'I'm afraid I don't have a husband,' she told him. 'I'm Alex Cameron.'

It was too much! For a moment he had a wild desire to shout his frustration. He clenched his teeth, feeling the tenseness of his jaw muscles, and made an effort to keep his voice cool and level. Aware that it sounded clipped and grudging and slightly pompous instead, he said, 'I beg your pardon. I was led to believe—that is, I assumed——'

She looked at him, her head slightly tipped to one side, waiting for him to finish. She wasn't going to help, obviously. There was still a faint smile on her lips that annoyed him intensely.

Dammit, it had been a natural enough assumption. She was a jade carver, and he'd been looking round the carving factories for days without seeing a single woman doing the work. When they told him that Alex Cameron was one of the best, they hadn't said anything about Cameron being a woman. He wasn't a male chauvinist, but no doubt she was militantly feminist, ready to pounce on any hapless man who make a simple mistake. He suddenly abandoned the apology and deliberately let his eyes rove over her again, blatantly noting the lack of make up and bra, the trendy 'ethnic' print on her skirt, the bare brown toes showing beneath it. 'I thought Alex was short for Alexander,' he said bluntly.

'Alexandra,' she said. She had stopped smiling, and there was a spark in her eyes, now. 'Everybody calls me Alex, Mr . . .?'

'Richard Lewis.'

'How do you do, Mr Lewis,' she said, so formally that he knew she was laughing at him again. In fact, her lips had regained their smiling curve, but the bright temper remained in her eyes. She put out her hand, and he automatically closed it in his, feeling the tensile strength of her long fingers, the smooth warmth of her skin, before she withdrew from his hard clasp. 'I'll bet no one ever calls you Dick,' she said.

So you want a fight, lady? he thought. Right, you've got it! The idea was immensely stimulating, the adrenalin suddenly shooting through his veins, making his heart hammer against his ribs and stifling his breathing. It only lasted for a moment, leaving him somewhat surprised. 'No, they don't,' he said. 'I don't like it.'

He saw the quick derision in her eyes and held

them with his, daring her to say what was in her mind. She had very beautiful eyes, lucid and unequivocal, with dark lashes that were golden on the curving tips. It gave him great satisfaction to read what she was thinking, to watch the mysterious pupils contract suddenly as she remembered that they had barely met, blinked and made her face into a mask of politeness.

'You wanted to see some of my work?' she asked.

'Yes. If I may?' The sarcasm was very slight, but her steady look told him she had noticed.

She shrugged and turned from him to lead the way into the house, pushing open the heavy door.

The passage he stepped into was dim and cool, with a polished wood floor and a couple of fringed, patterned mats. She opened a door on the right, and then they were in a long, well-lit room, once two rooms, he guessed, now converted into a workspace. The floor here was bare boards, unpolished and waterstained. There was a large diamond-edged circular saw in one corner. A strong bench held her tools and several pieces of stone in various stages, and smaller saws and polishing machines were clamped to its edge. He looked cursorily at all this, having seen similar set-ups before. His gaze lingered for a while on a large chunk of raw greenstone, looking like any ordinary riverbed stone, lying near the saw. Knowing how heavy the stuff was, he wondered if she was able to lift it herself.

'Over here,' she said, and he followed her to another table against one wall, on which stood a glass display case.

There wasn't a lot, but he could see at once that her work was outstanding. These pieces were

even better than the few samples in the shops he
had visited. Most of them were pendants. There
was one example of a wedge shape, in deepest
green, almost black, so highly polished that it
seemed to reflect light like a mirror. A slightly
lighter stone had been used for a miniature *mere*,
the much prized Maori ceremonial club. Several
fish-hook designs revealed in graceful curves the
special luminosity of the stone in shades ranging
from the most delicate pastel to the rich moss
green traditionally associated with New Zealand
greenstone—*pounamu* to the Maori, nephrite to
the geologist, and now known and sold as jade
equal to some of the finest in the world. There
was no sign of the ubiquitous *tiki* copied from
early Maori use, but he was fascinated by several
intricately fashioned ornaments which conformed
to no usual pattern, yet seemed to blend the ideas
of modern abstract design with styles that echoed
the formal swirls and balanced decorations of
traditional Maori art.

'Those,' he said, his finger stabbing at the
glass. 'Are they your own designs?'

'Yes.' She lifted the lid of the case, and he took
one of the jade pendants in his hand, rubbing a
thumb over the satin smoothness of the polished
surface, then holding it up to the light by the
cord on which it was suspended, watching the
play of light over the carved edges. He replaced it
and did the same with another, enjoying the feel
of the stone against his exploring fingers, and the
way each piece showed a unique shading of light
and depth, even though the day outside the
window was still overcast and dim.

Alex Cameron watched him for a while, and
then said, 'Is it jewellery you're after?'

He put down the piece he held and said,' Do you do larger carvings, too?'

She stood looking at him for a moment or two as though weighing him up. Then she said, 'Come with me.'

She led him across the passageway into a sitting room furnished with a worn settee, a restored rocking chair of nineteenth-century design, and some cushions with woven covers. In one corner was an old glass-fronted cupboard, in which stood a small collection of jade figures—a Chinese style 'goddess' with enigmatic eyes and lips, her dress swirling about her fluidly, and lotus blossoms lying at her feet; a small vase, delicate and elaborately carved with an abstract design vaguely reminiscent of some bird from mythical times, a yearning beak flowing straight into pinned wings which seemed straining to be free, mounted on a flowing series of interlocking stylised leaf-like shapes; a horse and foal, the foal lying trustingly in the curve of its mother's body as she nudged it, her nostrils exquisitely flared, so that her loving breath in its ear was almost tangible; a naked child that Richard realised with an odd shock of recognition was Jane. 'May I?' he murmured, aching to touch them.

She nodded, turned a key in the door of the cupboard and stepped aside, regarding him with curiosity as he stood absorbed in the visual beauty and the tactile pleasure of her creations.

He examined them one by one, leaving the vase and the miniature sculpture of Jane for last. The vase in his hand, he asked, 'How much do you want for this?'

'A lot.' The mockery was back in her voice, just faintly—barely perceptible—but there.

Without looking up, he said again, 'How much?'

When she told him, he wondered if she had set the price astronomically high just for him. He should have made her tell him how long she had spent on it, questioned whether it was worth what she asked. Instead, he said casually, 'I'll write you a cheque, okay?' As soon as he had said it, he was angry with himself. What was he doing, trying to impress this woman, show her he was someone to be reckoned with?

After the briefest hesitation, she said, 'Fine. If you have identification?'

He accorded her a brief, sardonic smile. 'Of course.' He picked up the figure of the naked child and asked, 'And this?'

He heard her draw in her breath. 'It isn't for sale,' she said swiftly. 'I'm sorry.'

He had known that she wouldn't sell it. The confirmation gave him an odd satisfaction. Still, he couldn't resist testing her. 'I'll give you twice what I'm paying for the other one,' he said.

'It's still not for sale.' She had quickly hidden the surprise in her face, but he didn't like what had replaced it. He realised that for a little while she had almost respected him, but that was gone, now. Her eyes were scornful.

Resisting the impulse to tell her that he didn't make a habit of throwing his money in people's teeth, he held out the vase to her. She took it from his hand and led the way back to the studio to wrap it in some tissue from a stack at the end of her workbench. He watched her long, capable fingers as she efficiently made a secure parcel and sealed it with sticky tape.

He wrote the cheque out, scribbled his address

on the back, and gave it to her with his bank card. She handed the card back after a brief glance, and turned over the cheque to read the address.

'Christchurch,' she said, and he thought he detected an unspoken, *I thought so*. She didn't ask if he was on holiday, or why he had come to the Coast. She stood waiting for him to go, the parcel still in her hand, ready to give it to him.

Instead he asked, 'Mind if I look around?'

'Go ahead. Do you want me to explain things to you?'

'I've been round some of the factories. Were you doing something when I arrived? Don't let me hold you up if you're working.'

'I don't work with an audience,' she said.

He didn't ask why not, but strolled about the big room, looking at the hose and drainage system for the cold water that kept the big circular blade cool when she was cutting a large block, then at the smaller saws and the dental drills and tools for shaping the pieces. He paused to look at but not touch the unfinished fish-hook pendant lying by one of the polishing wheels, then moved to a sheaf of templates used for guiding the cutting of shapes from slices of stone. He looked through them, and came to a sheet of drawings, designs carefully sketched, shaded so that they conveyed some idea of the finished product. He pored over them for some minutes.

'Do you always start with a drawing?' he asked.

She said, 'No. Usually it helps, but sometimes I just let the stone guide me.' She had put down the parcel and was standing with one hand on the workbench, watching him.

'How much of this sort of thing do you do?' he

asked, indicating the drawing of a gracefully looped and intertwined pattern.

'Not much. It takes a long time to do, and that makes it expensive. So there's not a great demand. The tourists who come to the Coast generally want just a nice souvenir, not a work of art.'

'You don't sell nice souvenirs here.'

Richard knew that she sold to the retailers in Hokitika and Greymouth. He had seen the pendants, the bracelets, the occasional *mere*, with her label on them.

'I sell them to the tourist shops,' she said. 'This is off the beaten track, I couldn't make a living from the trade I do here.'

'You might get an increase in custom if your sign was more prominent.'

'I'll cut the trees back,' she said vaguely.

He said, 'You don't really care, do you?' She didn't want people coming here, disturbing her at work. She was standing there resenting his presence, he was sure.

She sidestepped the question. 'Most of my customers have been told about me by someone. Who sent you?'

'A couple of people mentioned your name. Woudn't you rather be doing this—' he indicated the sheet of drawings in his hand '—than turning out souvenirs?'

'My souvenirs are good,' she said defensively. 'They're not cheap, badly-worked junk.'

'I know—I've seen them. I asked you a question.'

She stared at him, wary. 'Why?'

'I'm in the trade myself. I'm interested in good quality original carvings and jewellery, especially, at the moment, jade.'

'A buyer?'

He hesitated. 'Yes.'

He saw her look down at the cheque that was lying on the bench in front of her. His personal cheque, with his name printed on the form.

'I bought the vase for myself,' he said.

'So, who do you buy for?' she asked him.

'A group of shops—a small chain, I suppose you'd call it. In Christchurch, Dunedin and Wellington. C. W. Lewis & Son. Heard of it?'

Alex Cameron shook her head. 'You're the son?'

He acknowledged it with a nod. 'I have a special commission from a client. He's asked us to find someone to make a replica of this.'

Taking an envelope from his pocket, he handed her three coloured photographs, different views of a Chinese carving, a dragon with its supple body curling back on itself, with delicately complicated patterns etched into the jade. There were measurements pencilled on the coloured prints. She examined the pictures carefully.

'It's beautiful,' she said. 'Why does your client want it copied?'

'It's all above board,' he assured her. 'We know him well. This particular piece was stolen some years ago. He was fond of it for its aesthetic value, apart from the fact that it was worth a lot of money. He would like to replace it, even though a copy won't be quite the same as having the original. Can you do it?'

'I could,' she said briefly. 'But copying isn't what I usually do. I prefer to work on my own designs.' She made to hand back the photographs, but instead of taking them, Richard said, 'My client is prepared to pay very well for a good job.'

She hesitated, her eyes going again to the photographs. He allowed himself a cynical little smile. Money, the great persuader. She looked up again unexpectedly, catching the smile, and stared at him for several seconds before putting the photographs down rather deliberately on the bench.

He wondered what she was thinking. He couldn't guess, now, what was going on her mind. Finally she moved and began to speak. Then Jane came in, her bare feet almost soundless on the boards. 'Mum!' she was saying. 'It's the most fantastic car! You should *see*——'

'Don't interrupt, darling. We were talking,' her mother said, but she put out her hand and Jane went into the curve of her arm, and they stood there together facing Richard, giving him the curious sensation of being an outsider.

'Sorry,' Jane apologised quickly. She turned her face up to her mother's to whisper, 'But it's neat, Mum!'

The woman smiled down at her, putting a finger admonishingly over the child's lips, and when she lifted her head to look at Richard again, the smile lingered for a moment. He felt a sudden odd contraction of muscles deep in the pit of his stomach.

She seemed, now, to be expecting him to speak first. He said, 'I'd like you to do it for us.'

'I don't think so,' she said, apparently making up her mind. 'I work for myself, strictly. That's how I like it.'

His smile was impatient. 'Yes, I understand that. Doing a commission isn't going to rob you of your independence, is it? I was told that you do take work on commission quite often.'

'It depends,' she said, 'on who is doing the commissioning.'

His anger must have shown, because she said hastily, 'I mean, usually I know the person, or they're a friend of a friend. You know the sort of thing.'

'I'm a businessman, Mrs Cameron,' he said, more dryly than he had intended. 'I understood that you were in business yourself.'

'It's *Ms*, actually, and I don't need to do business with people I don't care for. Or take commissions I don't want.'

Of course it was Ms, he thought. He might have known. He suppressed the involuntary derisive curve of his mouth, and said, 'I wish you'd give it some thought. Of course, none of what you've shown me is quite as difficult as this,' he added smoothly, glancing at the photographs, 'But your work is excellent, and I'm sure you could manage to reproduce it quite faithfully.'

She stared at him coolly, and at first he thought he had hit home, but after a moment she gave a faintly sardonic smile of her own, and a little nod as though acknowledging a point. 'You're very persistent, Mr Lewis. And clever with it.'

'As I said, my client is prepared to spend money for what he wants. A down payment, if you like, or even a form of retainer, so that you needn't worry about an income while you complete the commission.'

'And did you come all the way from Christchurch just for him?'

'Largely. I did have other business to attend to,' Richard said shortly.

'High-powered clients you have,' she murmured.

Catching the note of irony, he said, 'Yes. And you'd better be glad that there are people like him with the money to buy the kind of things that people like you make.'

Her eyebrows went up. 'Oh, I'm glad, Mr Lewis. I'm a regular Pollyanna, believe me!'

He suppressed the desire to verbally slap her down, determined that she wasn't going to get the better of him. 'You can just about name your price,' he told her, 'within reason. If you'd like to give me a quote, I'll take it back to him.'

Jane watched them curiously, the eyes that were so like her mother's going from one face to the other. The woman shrugged, and at last, as though she just wanted to get rid of him, said, 'Let me think about it. I'll write to you.'

He knew with certainty that she wouldn't. She had his address on the back of his cheque, but he slipped a card from his wallet and put it down before her as he picked up the vase, leaving the photographs where she had put them. He felt frustrated and angry, more angry than the situation warranted. If she wanted to cut off her nose to spite her face, why should he care?

He did care, because her work was exquisite, faultless, and he loved the feel and shape of it, the sheer pleasure of looking at it. And because something in her challenged him.

On impulse, he said, 'I'll come back. Next week. Think it over.'

She wouldn't find it so easy, perhaps, to say no to his face, and it would give him another chance to persuade her.

Her eyes dilated a little in surprise, perhaps a

measure of apprehension. Her hand moved absently on her daughter's shoulder, then smoothed the tousled fair head against her breast.

Jane said, 'Thanks for letting me sit in the car. I didn't make it dirty.'

'It was already pretty dirty,' Richard said ruefully.

'But not inside. I wiped my feet first.'

'That was thoughtful of you.' He reached out his own hand to touch her cheek. 'Goodbye, Jane. I'll see you next week.'

' 'Bye.' She disengaged herself from her mother's encircling arm to accompany him out to the veranda. She was standing on the step waving as he drove away.

An unsatisfactory visit, he decided as he regained the road. Why was the woman so reluctant to commit herself? It didn't look as though she was doing all that well at the moment. A solo mother with a child to support, she should have jumped at the chance of making a decent sum of money, of having some sort of assured amount. He wondered what had happened to Jane's father. Remembering the strong, lightly tanned hand stroking the child's hair, he tried to recall if there had been a wedding ring on it.

He wasn't sure. He had not been concentrating on that, but on watching her face, trying to discover what she was thinking.

He supposed she valued her independence, saw herself as the self-sufficient earth-mother type. Perhaps she was afraid her artistic integrity would be threatened by financial security. A couple of the other artisans he had spoken to had expressed themselves vaguely along those lines. One had professed a desire to retreat from the twentieth century, back to the nineteenth. He lived in a barn of a house heated by smoky fireplaces and lit by kerosene lamps. Richard found it hard to sympathise with his viewpoint. One ought, he felt, to be able to live with and in the century into which one was born. He didn't see any particular virtue in opting out of society, or in trying to. If it was that bad, one should try to change things, surely, not simply ignore them.

There was a long black hair draped over the dashboard, and he picked it off with his fingers. Not Jane's, certainly. The horse's. It must have been on Jane's clothes when she got into the car. He pushed it into the ash tray. A nice kid, Jane. Her mother had looked very young to have a daughter that age. He hadn't thought about it before, but she was surely not much older than twenty-five. He remembered her standing on the veranda, looking down at him as he tried to wipe Casanova's salive off his jacket, his shoes oozing muddy water and his trousers dripping with it. No wonder she had wanted to laugh! The sense of humour that had deserted him at the time reasserted itself. He pictured the scene vividly in his mind, and his lips twitched. Altogether it had been pretty disastrous, but now he could suddenly see that it was funny, too. He laughed aloud and shook his head. He would have to phone his father and explain that he needed another week. Somehow he was going to get Alex Cameron to do this work for them. As the laughter died, his mouth and chin took on a set look, and his eyes hardened. Richard Lewis rarely failed to get what he wanted.

CHAPTER TWO

ALEX picked up the photographs and slowly looked through them again. The carving was exquisite, and the photographer had recaptured clearly the pale, luminous quality of the jade. The stone might have been jadeite, highly prized by the Chinese, and not found in New Zealand. But an acceptable replica could be reproduced using a good quality 'Inanga' nephrite which was also light-coloured. Or—she recalled seeing a particularly fine pendant by a local artist using a very translucent stone from the Taramakau River . . .

Impatiently, she put the photographs down. Copying wasn't her thing, as she had told the Lewis man. Let him come back next week if he liked. If he wasted another journey, it was hardly her fault.

Dabbing resin on to the end of a three-inch dopstick, she fixed it to the back of the unfinished fish-hook and put it into the small oven for a few minutes to temporarily set the glue, so that she would be able to hold the small piece of jade by the stick while she polished it. Waiting for it to dry, she found her eyes straying to the pictures on the bench again. Whoever carved the dragon had been a master craftsman. The curled lips gave an impression that fire was just about to issue from the throat, and there was muscular power in the haunches. Alex snatched the photographs up, ready to stuff them into the envelope he had left, but the curve of the tail caught her eye, then the beauty of the patterns traced along the spine. She carried the envelope and the pictures absentmindedly with her over to the little oven, and propped them against the wall at the back of the table before removing the fish-hook from the heat.

The hook had been cut from a slice of greenstone, at first crudely with a smaller diamond-edged saw than the big one which had been used for the original slicing into the raw stone, and then with a profile wheel which followed the pattern she had pre-set for it. Then she had used a diamond-tipped 'dental' drill to carve into the curve of the hook, and to make a hole for threading a thong by which it could hang, and the edges had been painstakingly wet-sanded with fine paper. Now, once the dopstick cooled, she was ready to give the piece a final polish, using zinc oxide and small polishing wheels covered with leather.

The work was peculiarly soothing, although it also took very careful concentration. As she watched the lustre coming up on the jade, Alex felt her inexplicable tension begin to fade.

Something about that man had upset her equilibrium. At first she had been merely amused as she saw the stranger in his city clothes, obviously annoyed at having got them dirty, looking totally out of his element. A few minutes later she had realised that he was looking at her with a disdain that she hadn't cared for. He thought her a slob—or was the word slut, for the female gender?

She grinned a little. He wasn't bad looking, in a stuffy sort of way. She'd take a bet that he liked his women groomed and glamorised, with high-heeled shoes and not a hair out of place.

She pushed back her own hair, bending closer to the wheel as it whirred around, her fingers deftly moving the piece of jade from side to side to give it a smooth, even sheen. There had been more than a hint of red in his dark brown hair, and for a mere second or so she had seen a tiger gleam of temper in his eyes. Unusual eyes, not brown, not gold, but something in between. She had a piece of polished petrified wood that colour.

There was nothing petrified about Mr Lewis. In either sense. Smooth, classy, obviously used to getting his own way, he had been. And nobody called him Dick. She shouldn't have made that crack, of course. She didn't know why she had, except she had wanted to needle him, because he had made her aware of her bare feet and her old clothes, and that he didn't think much of her as a woman.

Good lord, she wasn't in that competition any more. Her clothes were comfortable and clean and she didn't need any man judging her desirability. It wasn't an issue, since she'd decided that she could live without men. Life, she had discovered, was easier and simpler without complicated relationships with the other sex.

'Did that man buy the vase?' Jane asked that evening, as she noted the empty space in the corner cupboard.

'Yes, he did.' Alex looked up from the book she was reading to smile at her daughter, who was sprawled on the floor, elbows resting on one of the woven cushions while she read her own book.

'How much?' Jane asked, and whistled when Alex told her. 'That's an awful lot, isn't it?'

'Enough to buy a new sofa, I should think,' Alex answered, shifting a little as she felt one of the springs trying to force its way through the worn upholstery.

Jane laughed at her pained expression. 'Is he a rich tourist?'

'He's a businessman.'

'What does that mean?'

'He owns a shop—at least, he and his father do. They buy things and then sell them to other people.'

'Sounds boring,' Jane pronounced.

'Agreed. But maybe he doesn't think it's boring. After all, I buy and sell things, too.'

'You buy stone and then sell it when you've made it into something. That's different. How come you sold him the vase?'

'Well, he—liked it.'

'That other man that came last Easter liked it, too, but you told him none of those things were for sale. I heard you.'

'Don't sound so accusing, Jane! I changed my mind, that's all.'

'I thought you didn't like him.'

'Who?'

'The man who came today. When you were talking to him in the studio, I thought—I dunno—just that you didn't like him much.'

'I didn't, particularly.'

'Well, why did you sell him the vase, then?'

Alex looked at her daughter helplessly. She didn't really know why she had sold the vase to

Richard Lewis. It was true that she had already refused it to someone else. The man had come looking for a bargain in jade and had made it plain that he regarded his purchase as a hedge against inflation, holding forth at length about how he had learned that Westland jade was a diminishing resource, and how his business acumen had led him to invest in some fine jade pieces on which he hoped eventually to make a handsome profit. He had come with a mutual acquaintance, and after selling him several of her pendants, Alex had invited them both into the sitting room for coffee. And politely refused to sell him one of her jade carvings, grateful to the friend who had brought him for not batting an eyelid. It was very unbusinesslike of her, but she preferred that the larger carvings, which took her many hours to make, and were the product of her mind and heart as much as of her clever fingers, should go to people who would love them for themselves rather than for their monetary worth.

And Richard Lewis had handled them with a lover's touch—firm and gentle, his fingers tracing their outlines with a tactile appreciation. She had been impressed by that.

'He made me an offer I couldn't refuse,' she said lightly. 'Okay?'

'Phoo!' said Jane. 'You must have liked him a bit, after all. Anyway, I thought he was neat.'

'You thought his car was neat,' Alex murmured.

'Is he coming back next Saturday? Do you think he'd let me have a ride in it?'

'No, I don't. And you're not to ask him! That's an order.'

'Okay, okay. What's he coming back for?'

'To try and twist my arm, I suspect.'

Jane wrinkled her nose. 'You mean, make you do something you don't want to?'

'Mmm.'

'Why don't you want to do it?'

'Because it's copying someone else's work.'

'Like a forgery?'

Alex laughed. 'No, not really. More like apprentice painters used to do—copying something of the master's before they were allowed to go on to higher things.'

'That dragon, you mean?'

'That's right.'

'I think it'd be fun. It's a beaut dragon.'

'Yes, it is.'

It was, and Alex found herself looking at the photographs often. Every morning she promised herself she was going to slide them back into their envelope and put it aside for the Lewis man. But every time she made to do so, the sheer pleasure of looking at them stopped her. It wouldn't hurt to leave them there until he came. The Chinese had been masters of the art of jade carving for centuries; she had seen some of their work in museums, and often daydreamed about some day having enough money to go to Hongkong, where there were still jade carvers plying their ancient trade.

The Maoris had had their own methods of dealing with the stone, painstaking and time-consuming, and considering the limitations imposed on the early carvers by their primitive materials, it was amazing what results they had achieved. Most of the precious *pounamu* had been used for *meres*, the ceremonial hand weapons carried by chiefs, but some smaller pieces had been made into chisels and other tools before the advent of iron brought from Europe, and some had been carved into the grotesque shape of the *tiki* representing the first man, or the beautifully ornamental *pekapeka*, once used for keeping apart the hooks on a fishing line. From being useful articles hung on thongs round the neck as a convenient way of ensuring they were always to hand, the *pekapeka* had gradually evolved into purely ornamental objects for which there was a great demand. Even today many Maoris, as well as some Pakehas who often had no idea of their true significance, liked to wear a greenstone ornament. Alex had been pleased and proud when a Maori *kuia* came and asked her to make a six-hole *pekapeka*. The commission had made her nervous, too, but the old lady had been satisfied, and ordered more work. She was Alex's most regular and most valued client.

On Saturday the morning was beautiful, the sun warm and lazy, and the bellbirds in the trees behind the house began calling the day to each other at first light.

Alex found herself staring into her wardrobe, surveying the meagre collection of clothing with a dissatisfied eye. When it dawned on her what she was doing, she gave a smothered exclamation of disgust, and grabbed the first items to hand—a pair of faded denims and a bodyshirt that had been unsuccessfully tie-dyed to a rather splotchy green and white, in the days when a friend who was keen on the art had persuaded her to try refurbishing her clothes that way.

She brushed her hair until it shone softly. The ritual always woke her up and made her feel fresh

and tingly, and able to face anything the day
might bring.

When it brought Richard Lewis, she was ready
for him, but since he didn't arrive until nearly
twelve, she had almost decided he wasn't coming
after all, and prolonged anticipation had somehow
dulled the edge of her slightly militant mood. In
fact, to her own annoyance, she felt almost
relieved to see him at last.

She had heard the car arrive, and Jane's voice,
followed by his deeper tones, but the words
didn't carry to the studio. She knew Jane would
bring him in, and went on carefully hand-
polishing an oval-shaped cabuchon of jade which
she planned to set into a necklace. For the tourist
trade, and the hell with Mr Lewis and his
supercilious hints about it.

Jane came in first, her eyes brilliant with
excitement. 'Mum, Mr Lewis said he'll take me
over to the mine in his car! It's all right, isn't it?'

'Jane!'

'I didn't ask him, honestly, *truly*! I didn't, did
I?' she appealed to Richard.

'Certainly not,' he agreed promptly. 'It was a
completely spontaneous offer on my part.'

'You said I could go to the mine, today,' Jane
reminded her. 'I promised Paddy I'd come. He's
expecting lots of visitors this afternoon, and he
needs me and Shawn to help with the pans.'

'After lunch,' Alex reminded her. 'And I
thought you were going on Casanova?'

'I'll have a sandwich while you talk to Mr
Lewis, and then he can take me——'

'No, Jane, I don't think so.'

'Oh, Mu-um!'

Richard said, 'I don't mind, really.'

'Please, Mum?'

Alex bit her lip. She had tried to bring up Jane with as few rules as possible, but the ones she had were supposed to be regarded as pretty well unbreakable. 'Darling,' she said, 'we have a rule, remember?'

Jane looked puzzled, then burst out, 'About going in cars——? But—Mr Lewis isn't a stranger. You know him!'

'Not very well,' Alex argued, the man's incredulous eyes on her making her cheeks uncomfortably warm.

'But——'

'Perhaps you'd like to come along for the ride,' Richard broke in, speaking to Alex. 'Wouldn't that solve the problem?'

She looked at the gleam of sardonic humour in his eyes, and the anxious pleading in Jane's, and said weakly. 'Thank you. All right.'

Jane threw her arms around her mother's neck, and then danced off to the kitchen to make herself a sandwich, leaving an uncomfortable silence behind her.

Richard Lewis was lounging against the workbench, and Alex realised that today he had left the city suit behind and was wearing fitting beige designer slacks and a knit shirt in a lighter beige, with slip-on shoes that were not quite moccasins. He looked expensively casual and as well co-ordinated as an ad for a menswear store. But the less formal clothes revealed a surprisingly strong-looking masculine body beneath them that she had not noticed in the sober suit.

He said softly, 'I'm not, actually, a child molester.'

'I'm sure you're not, Mr Lewis. But with

children some rules are important. Making exceptions confuses the issue for them, so it's best to be quite clear-cut. Jane isn't to go in a car with anyone I don't know well. Do you have a daughter?'

'No. I'm not married.'

Alex couldn't suppress a flicker of curiosity. He must be at least thirty, probably a bit more. He had good looks, money and a certain attraction. Many women would probably jump at the chance of marrying him.

Her eyes must have lingered, speculating, for too long. She saw his brows come together suddenly, and looked away. 'I'm sorry if Jane was dropping hints,' she said. 'She's mad about cars.'

'She only dropped one small hint—and I needn't have taken her up on it. I don't normally do things I don't want to do.'

It was her cue, but for some reason she let it pass. She turned vaguely in the direction of the photographs he had left, about to pick them up and hand them back, but he forestalled her, reaching across to gather them up in his long fingers. She caught the faint scent of pine aftershave, felt his sleeve brush against her arm as she withdrew her own tentatively outstretched hand.

'Sorry,' he said, smiling down at her. She was hemmed in somehow between him and the table, and for a moment he just stood there, too close. Alex had a sudden conviction that he had done it on purpose, indulging in a masculine game to test her susceptibility.

Her eyes sparkled angrily. He lifted his brows slightly and stepped back without haste, allowing her to move away from him and breathe more freely.

'I see you've been studying these,' he said, nothing in his voice, in his face, but polite enquiry and professional interest. She was imagining things, she thought confusedly. The wordless exchange *had* affected her, to her chagrin, but he was showing no sign of awareness.

'Yes,' she said, steadying her voice. 'Jane says it's a beaut dragon.'

'She's right. Isn't she?'

'Oh, yes. Look, Mr Lewis, I don't want to waste your——'

But he wasn't listening. His voice cut smoothly across hers. 'I'm glad you think so. You'll understand why my client is so fond of it. He's an elderly gentleman, and the theft was particularly mean. Since he got the idea of having a replica made, he's had almost a new lease of life.'

She opened her mouth to speak, but he was looking at the top picture in his hand, saying, 'I don't have the talent, unfortunately, to do anything like this, but if I did, I think that I would feel—challenged by the opportunity. I'd like to know if I could make as good a job of it as the original artist did. I'd want to try, at least. If I had the ability.'

It was exactly how Alex had begun to feel, herself.

'I'm not a copyist,' she said feebly.

Richard looked at her, his eyes suddenly hard. 'What do you call these?' he demanded, going over to the case where she displayed her pendants. 'This chisel-shape here, and this fish-hook, and this dog-tooth? And what about these bracelets

and necklaces? Oh, I'll admit a dazzling crafts-
manship which gives them your individual stamp,
and some quirks of design in a few of them which
show originality, but the Maoris were turning out
these pendant things hundreds of years back, and
the shops are full of them, now. Even the
necklaces and bracelets are only variations on
European designs.'

'That's different!' she protested. 'They're my
bread-and-butter lines. Everyone makes something like that.'

'Well, you don't have to!' he told her. 'Not as
long as you're making this!' He thrust the
photographs towards her. 'I tell you, we'll keep
you in bread-and-butter, and jam, too, if
necessary, until it's finished.'

She backed up against the bench, putting her
hands behind her almost as if to stop herself from
taking the pictures from him.

'He's an old man,' Richard said persuasively.
'He's decided to have this done before he dies.
It's become a sort of last project. I want him to
have the best.'

She looked up from the photographs, caught
by the sincerity of his tone, and saw that it was in
his face, too. His eyes pleaded and demanded at
the same time. His mouth was set stubbornly, but
she could see now that it wasn't simply that he
was determined to beat her down until she agreed
to do what he wanted.

'You really care, don't you?' she asked almost
accusingly. 'It isn't just a business deal, with a fat
commission.'

His hand holding the photographs dropped,
and he shrugged. 'Not entirely. He's a nice old
boy, and I'd like to do this for him.'

He held out the pictures. Alex took them from him in silence, her eyes captured by his.

'You're the carver I want,' he said. 'I promise you, you won't lose anything by it.'

She wondered if he was being terribly clever at her expense, playing on her sympathy. And at the same time she felt oddly guilty, because she knew that all week she had been fighting the temptation to take the job, that she had felt the challenge of trying to equal the master. What had held her back was really just her own odd reaction to Richard Lewis. That first time she had read a subliminal warning in his eyes when she had deliberately annoyed him. It wasn't that any man had the power to frighten her. The threat was more subtle than that, nothing more than a slight, uneasy ripple across the tranquil surface of her life. It was in the involuntary quickening of her pulses when he had leaned close to her today, in the sudden rush of unwarranted antaganism she had felt last week when he looked into her eyes and dared her to laugh at him, making her want quite fiercely to laugh in his face and see what he was going to do about it. It was a curious kind of sexual awareness, and if she had had any doubts last time they met, she had none now.

She could do without that. Her life was just fine and dandy as it was, and Richard Lewis was a boat-rocker. A man like that was the last thing she needed at this stage.

But she did want to do this, and he lived in Christchurch, after all. She had the photographs, and once they had agreed on the financial arrangements and she gave him an estimate of the time and costs involved, he would go away. She

need never see him again. He was just a glorified
messenger boy for this other man, the client.

'All right,' she said. 'I'll do it—for him.'

His eyes glinted briefly as he noted her
wording. But all he said was, 'Good. I know he'll
be pleased.'

Jane came in with half a sandwich in one hand
and an apple in the other. Alex cast her a warning
glance, and she stood in the doorway, her eyes on
Richard.

'Ready?' He smiled at her as she nodded, a
mouthful of sandwich bulging in her cheek.

'Finish your sandwich,' Alex said resignedly.
'Paddy won't have had lunch, yet, anyway.' She
winced as Jane hurriedly stuffed the rest of the
bread and cheese into her mouth, and resolved
that later on she would have a private talk with
her daughter about manners.

In the car Jane bounced on to the back seat,
and Alex sat beside Richard. It was only a five-
minute journey, and they were soon turning in at
the mine gate. Three cars were parked there, and
a group of people were standing around the
young giant Richard had spoken to the first time
he came there, listening to him. As the group
broke apart and moved towards the cars, the man
looked up and, seeing Jane scrambling out of the
Mercedes, lifted a hand in greeting and came
striding over.

'You're arriving in style,' he commented to the
child. 'Shawn isn't here yet.' Turning to the
adults he said 'Hi, Alex,' and bent a curious blue
gaze on Richard. 'G'day. I see you found her all
right.'

'This is Mr Lewis,' said Jane. 'This is Paddy,
Mr Lewis. I mean this is Mr Patrick Finnerty.'

She looked at her mother for approval, and Alex gave her a smiling nod as Paddy offered a large, calloused paw through the driver's window to Richard.

'Name's Paddy,' he drawled.

'Richard,' the other man conceded politely. Alex hid a smile as he retrieved his hand and flexed it surreptitiously. Paddy was a gentle lamb in giant's clothing, but he didn't know his own strength.

'Thanks for delivering the hired help,' said Paddy, ruffling Jane's hair so that she looked more boyish than ever. 'Like to look around? You didn't have time the other day. It's on the house.'

'Well, thank you,' Richard began, 'but——'

'You can pan for gold,' Jane told him. 'It's neat fun. I'll show you, if you like.'

'Thank you, Jane, but I——'

'Come on!' she said excitedly, and swung open his door. Alex looked at him covertly, wondering what he would do. In a spirit of mischief, she murmured, 'I'm in no hurry to get back, if you'd like to try your luck.'

'You're welcome to have a go,' said Paddy, and Jane plucked at Richard's sleeve. 'I know how to do it. It's really easy, honest!'

He cast a hard glance at Alex, who was biting hard on her lower lip and avoiding his eyes. 'All right,' he said, getting out of the car, 'I'll have a go.'

Jane took his hand and dragged him across the car-park to the cottage, dived inside, and came back with two shallow tin pans, one of which she handed to him. 'There are lots of tunnels about that the miners made,' she told him. 'You can see the entrance of one from here.' She pointed along a worn track and uphill, and he saw a narrow, dark entrance among the scrubby growth. 'Want to see?'

He didn't, particularly, but she was obviously dying to show him, so he consented to be led several yards into the tunnel and out again. But as it was low and he had to stoop to walk in it, he declined to visit any more.

'That's Happy Jack's claim over there,' she told him, pointing to the rusted remains of a sluice race, and a pile of stones damming a small stream. 'He was panning and sluicing here until just after the war. He was very old, even then. But this is where Paddy's sluicing now.' He followed her as she clambered over a ridge. At the top she turned and made some pantomime gestures, looking beyond him. Paddy was still standing by the car, and Alex had got out and was beside him. Richard saw Paddy wave and nod to Jane, and she said, 'Goody, he said we can start the sluice. You'll have to help me with the pump.'

'Oh, will I?' Richard murmured, looking at the contraption like an outsize fireman's hose that stood on a rusting framework before them. It pointed at a washed-out cliff at the foot of which was a rubbly heap of rock and mud.

'Just push the pump handle down and up a few times,' Jane instructed, showing him the action.

Richard meekly complied, and was rewarded in a short time by a roaring burst of water shooting from the nozzle of the hose straight at the cliff. Stones and mud were immediately washed down and ran with the surplus water through a narrow race dug into the ground and heading downhill to the stream.

'You can turn it in different directions!' Jane yelled above the noise of the water, and moved the nozzle slightly so that the jet of water was propelled at another area. 'Come and see!' She left the hose and led him to a narrow bridge spanning the race, watching the muddy rubble wash through it, bouncing over a grid that lined the race. When the water pressure died to a trickle she said, 'See, the gold is heavier than the stones, so it sinks through the grid and gets caught underneath in a layer of hessian, and every few weeks Paddy lifts the grid and gets the gold out.'

'No nuggets?' Richard queried, intrigued in spite of himself.

'Oh, no. Just dust and flakes. Paddy says hardly anyone finds nuggets now. The gold seams were pretty well worked out in the nineteenth century. Come and get some grit, and I'll show you how to pan. Paddy's got the tubs over there,' she pointed to a series of water-filled containers fixed at waist-height under a tin roof on poles, 'but it's more fun in the stream.'

Taking his pan, she scrambled down the bank to the head of the race, and heaped a few handfuls of spoil into each. Then she took him to the stream, and kicked off her shoes to stand at the edge of the water. Gingerly, he planted his own feet just on dry land.

'Like this.' Jane dipped the pan in the stream and began swirling the water about in it, letting some of the mud and small stones float away as she did so.

Trying to follow her example, Richard took first too little water, and then too much, but in a few minutes started to get the feel of the motion. He hadn't expected to find any gold at all, but,

just as he began to get bored with the whole
process, Jane, who had been keeping a critical eye
on him even while she worked her own pan,
pointed and said, 'There, see, you've got some
colour.'

'I have?' Sceptically, he looked more closely at
the little remaining dirt in his pan, and caught a
gleam of greenish yellow.

'Careful, now,' said Jane. 'Very gently. Like
this, see?'

She took the pan from him, dipped it again
with caution, and showed him how to let the
stones and mud tip out. The yellow gleam
became brighter, and she handed him back the
pan, watching as he followed her instructions
until he had perhaps half a teaspoon of the
precious metal sitting snugly in the curve of the
pan.

'Of course, there's a lot of other stuff mixed
with it,' the child told him knowledgeably. 'You
can get the iron out with a magnet, if you like,
but to get real, pure gold, you have to treat it
with mercury. Shall I get you a bottle to put it
in?'

'Thank you,' he said gravely. Straightening up,
he realised that he had been bending for a long
time, and put a hand to his back to ease the
stiffness as he turned towards the path. Reaching
the ridge, he could see Paddy still talking to Alex,
she leaning against the door and he with his hand
on the top, his head bent to her as she laughed up
into his face.

'What about yours?' Richard asked Jane,
looking back at her.

'Oh, that's all right, I can finish my panning
later.' She led the way to the house and found a

glass phial into which she carefully funnelled his few grains of gold, then corked it and handed to him.

'It's fun, isn't it?' She grinned up at him, and he laughed and said, 'Yes, it's a lot of fun. Thank you very much, Jane.'

'Thanks for the ride.' As they crossed the car-park again, she said, 'Here's Shawn. And Greyboy.'

Greyboy, Richard surmised, must be the horse the child was riding, a short-backed, barrel-shaped little pony in marked contrast to Jane's huge rawboned Casanova. The boy who slid off its back was black-haired and olive-skinned, but his eyes were a clear, light grey. He was slightly shorter than Jane, but they were obviously kindred spirits, because he left the horse, its rope rein looped on its back, to its own devices, and made a beeline for the Mercedes, an interested glow in his eyes.

He was circling the car with the air of a connoisseur by the time they reached it, and Jane said, 'It's Mr Lewis's. I got a ride in it.'

Shawn gave her an envious look and asked, 'What's it like?'

'Pretty good. The seats are all smooth and squishy.'

Paddy and Alex straightened away from the car, and Alex said, 'I think we'd better be moving, or you'll be conned into giving Shawn a ride, too.' To Paddy she added, 'Mr Lewis is what's known as a soft touch.'

Paddy cast him a speculative look and said, 'Doesn't look it to me.' Richard was looking at Alex; his mouth smiling but his eyes narrowed at the hint of mockery in hers.

Paddy said, 'I'll bring Jane home for you. Thanks for letting her come.'

'Do they really help?'

'Sure they do. On a busy day they can be pretty handy, washing the pans and giving out the torches for the tunnels, not to mention keeping an eye on the ticket office when I'm demonstrating the sluice. I ought to be paying them.'

'They're quite happy with washing for free gold. Jane's got nearly an eggcup full.'

'She's a great little worker. Hello.' Paddy turned as a car drove slowly over the cattle-stop, his eyes brightening. 'More visitors. The afternoon rush is about to begin.'

'We'll be off, then,' said Alex. 'Good luck.'

'See you, Alex. Good to meet you, Richard. Drop by again.' He opened the passenger door for her, and Richard got into his own seat and started the engine.

'You don't mind Paddy driving Jane home,' he said as he negotiated the cattle-stop.

'Paddy's a friend. And the only man I completely trust.'

He looked at her sharply, but returned his gaze to the road before he queried, 'Why don't you trust men?'

She shrugged. 'I just told you, I trust Paddy.'

'As an exception. Men in general you don't trust.' She didn't answer, and he drove the rest of the way in silence.

She got out without waiting for him. He followed her up the steps to the veranda.

'We have some arrangements to make,' he reminded her.

'I know. You'd better stay for lunch,' she said,

glancing at the man's watch which was strapped to her wrist.

'I've had more pressing invitations,' he murmured, his eyebrows slightly raised.

Her shoulders lifted briefly, and she met his eyes for a long moment. She hadn't intended to be rude and she was damned well not apologising. If he wanted to take it that way, then let him. 'I'm making lunch,' she said. 'You're welcome to stay if you want to.'

Richard went to the kitchen with her, and leaned against the scrubbed pine table, surveying the big, cool room with interest. Alex had stripped the layers of paint off the original wood and applied a clear satin finish to the walls and cupboards, laid a tile-patterned vinyl on the floor and hung orange and white gingham curtains at the window. The old coalburning stove still stood in a white-painted brick alcove, a copper kettle gleaming on its surface, but a modern electric cooker and a refrigerator were placed against one of the walls near the sink. On a wide mantel over the old stove a collection of black iron kitchen utensils made an unusual decorative touch against the natural wood of the wall. Alongside them were plant-pots holding mint, parsley and thyme, and from hooks on the underside of the shelf hung wicker containers for onions and garlic.

'This is a very pleasant room,' he said.

'Thank you.' She opened the refrigerator, taking out a lettuce to wash it at the sink, then deftly tearing the leaves and arranging them in a bowl. She took a bottle of dressing from a cupboard, dribbling it over the crisp pieces, then went to the refrigerator again for cucumber and an apple which she sliced on top of the lettuce.

On top of that again she spooned out a generous amount of cottage cheese, and finally grated some walnuts over the white curd before garnishing it with quarters of orange.

'Can I do something?' asked Richard, as she placed the attractive result in the centre of the table.

'There are plates in that cupboard over there,' she told him, pointing. 'And knives and forks in the drawer underneath it.'

He found the blue and white striped china and the stainless steel cutlery, and set two places, while she placed an oiled teak breadboard on the table and began slicing a whole-grain loaf.

'We eat vegetarian,' she said. 'I hope you don't mind.'

'Not at all,' he said, but she had caught the look of resignation on his face as he took the wooden chair opposite her.

'This is delicious,' he admitted, after a few mouthfuls, and she smiled demurely at him, not missing the note of surprise.

He actually had two helpings before she made coffee, which he accepted with well concealed apprehension.

'It's all right,' she assured him. 'It's pure instant out of a jar, not made with dock leaves or anything.'

He acknowledged the comment with a wry smile. 'I admit I wondered.'

'Not all vegetarians are health food freaks,' she said.

'So why are you a vegetarian?'

'I think we can get by without killing other creatures for food.'

'It's not a religious belief?'

She shook her head. 'Just a personal principle. I don't believe in killing.'

'Then you're a pacifist, too?'

'That's right. All the way.'

He looked at her consideringly, and she looked back with a blend of defiance and the subtle mockery that challenged him. 'You think I'm a nutter, don't you?' she asked.

'No. An idealist, perhaps.'

'But you'd go to war for a principle?'

'I'd go to almost any lengths to avoid war,' he said slowly. 'But what would *you* have done when Hitler was killing six million Jews, not to mention a few million other innocent non-combatants?'

'That's a tricky one,' she admitted. 'But there should have been another way. Not one that committed millions of people to a war which caused even more deaths.'

'Should have been—okay. In a perfect world there would have been, but as things stood what other way was there?'

'Maybe there was no other way, then. But it was a tragic, wasteful way, and there must have been a way to prevent it before it happened, if only someone had seen and acted on it. We ought to be able to do better, now.'

'Ah,' he said. 'That's begging the question. Should, ought—when it comes to the actual point, often there is no choice . . .'

They argued for ages, Richard making points with provocative deliberation, and Alex passionately defending her own views with skill and logic.

At last he said, 'Obviously we could go on like this for hours, and neither of us will convince the other. Shall we start talking business?'

'Yes, of course,' she agreed swiftly. 'I can give you an estimated price, but I don't have the right stone in the studio at the moment. I can't tell how long it will be before I find one. And once the word is out that I'm looking for a particular stone the price may well go up.'

'You don't collect your own?'

She shook her head. 'I don't own a claim. Jane and I fossick sometimes, everyone does, but by the measurements scribbled on those photos, I'm going to have to start with a good-sized piece, and I can't just go and help myself. In any case, I'd need to be very lucky to find just the right one. I'll have to contact prospectors and hope one of them will bring it in for me.'

'All right. I'll give you a deposit on the deal, and perhaps you can let me know when you get the stone. I'd like to see it.'

Alex hadn't bargained on this. 'Is that necessary?'

'I'm sure it isn't. I'm not questioning your judgment. But I'd like to see the work in its different stages. It would interest me, and my client would like me to report back. He doesn't travel, himself, any more.'

'You haven't told me who he is.'

'Does it matter? You're not likely to know him.'

'I'd like to know his name. Unless it's a secret.'

'He wouldn't want it spread all over, but his name's Mason—Gerald Mason. He used to be a judge, and before that he was a brilliant lawyer. He's old, now, but he has one of the most razor-sharp minds I've ever encountered.'

'And he likes beautiful things.'

'He does, indeed.' Richard smiled faintly. 'He

still isn't past liking beautiful women, either. His wife is half his age, and a looker as well. She's his third.'

Alex didn't smile, and he looked at her quizzically. 'You don't approve?'

'It's nothing to do with me.'

'You're jumping to conclusions, though. He isn't a roué, and she didn't marry him for his money or his position. They like each other very much—I suspect they're still in love.'

'That's very nice,' Alex said politely, and began gathering up the plates.

Richard took out his cheque book and scribbled on it. When he gave her the slip of paper she glanced at it, and then looked again. It was very generous for a deposit. 'Thank you,' she said.

He stood looking down at her, his gaze sober, and suddenly intent. 'What happened to your husband?' he asked.

Her face remained perfectly calm, and she answered him without hesitation. 'I never had one,' she said. 'I wasn't married to Jane's father.'

CHAPTER THREE

RICHARD felt jolted. Jolted and inexplicably angry, and although he tried to hide it, he knew that Alex thought he was shocked. Her eyes were bitterly derisive as she watched his face, and even her mouth took on a hint of a satirical curve.

He saw himself suddenly through her eyes, conservative, middle-class and slightly superior, and he curbed a savage desire to wipe the smile off her face with some crushing remark.

Instead he said merely, 'I see.' And knew that it came out clipped and disapproving, confirming her judgment of him.

One of her shoulders lifted in a small, uncaring shrug, dismissing him and his opinions. He wanted to bombard her with questions he had no right to ask, and felt the frustrating weight of the conventions that made them unaskable.

'Well,' she said, 'I'll let you know when I've located a suitable stone. Thank you for your confidence, Mr Lewis.'

She began moving towards the front door, forcing him to follow. On the veranda she waited for him to go down the steps to his car, her thumbs hooked into the pockets of her faded jeans in a way that reminded him of Jane.

He stopped at the top of the steps and held out his hand to her. 'Thank you for taking the job,' he said.

She put her hand in his and he felt with a keen, unexpected pleasure the strength and feminine shape of her fingers. Holding them, he looked down and turned her hand curiously in his grip as he noticed the satin gleam of her thumbnail.

Following his gaze she smiled and said, 'Jade workers don't need nail polish.'

The polishing wheel, of course. As she moved the small pieces against the leather, and it brushed her nails, it imparted this surprising gloss. He smiled back and released her hand slowly. On his way back to the town, he flexed his fingers on the steering wheel, and in imagination he could still feel the tensile warmth of hers.

It was several weeks before a suitable piece of stone turned up. The word was out, and Alex waited for one of the local prospectors to come up with a find. Jane and Shawn entered into the hunt, fossicking at the weekends on the claim that legally belonged to Shawn's people. The Terawitis were an old West Coast family, an interesting mixture of Maori and Irish, the clan encompassing the fair hair and blue eyes of Paddy Finnerty, and the dark copper skin, brown eyes and coal black hair of Shawn's father, Paddy's second cousin, as well as all shades in between. A complicated pattern of relationships had emerged from a great deal of intermarrying since the nineteenth-century gold-rush days when a wild Irish prospector had first met and married a dark-haired, melting-eyed Maori girl.

Shawn, like many of the local Maori youngsters, was an expert jade spotter. A river stone that the neophyte would pass without a second glance might catch his eye and prove to be greenstone disguised by the typical rough crust that encased the precious jade. And he had taught Jane how to wade in likely streams, feeling with her feet for the tell-tale soapy texture of a jade pebble or rock. Much of what they turned up was of low quality, and most finds were small, not particularly valuable. But they had a great deal of fun, and Alex would pay the Terawiti family a small sum for any jade they collected that was of use to her, and give 'prospectors' wages' to the children.

Once she had made up her mind to do the dragon, Alex found herself impatient to start the work, and twice when prospectors brought in lumps of stone that looked promising, she had to tamp down her excitement before critically examining what they had to show her. One proved to be too dark, and the other was fatally flawed, with a series of grainy lines which would make it difficult to work and spoil the finished product. Reluctantly, she sent them away. It might be months before a suitable piece was available.

She went to the jade factories to see what they had, thinking she might be able to buy a piece from them. Sometimes they bought huge boulders of jade which were occasionally discovered far upriver. The finds might be so large that a saw was transported there to make the first cut to determine quality, and then to slice the jade into manageable pieces which would be lifted out by helicopter. But even here Alex drew a blank. No such stone had been brought in for some time, and what was left of previous ones was not what she was looking for.

Then Jane came flying into the studio on the last day of term, just before Christmas, saying, 'Mum, Matty gave me a lift from the school bus stop, and she's got an enormous bit of stone for you! Come and see.'

Matty Yovic had emigrated from Yugoslavia as a girl, to marry the childhood sweetheart who had preceded her to New Zealand. Her husband had died young, leaving Matty to carry on the prospecting he had been engaged in, and now in her sixties she was one of the most experienced prospectors in the business. She stood on the veranda, sagging woollen trousers tucked into muddy gumboots, a faded plaid bush shirt tied about the waist with a piece of baling twine, and a stained felt hat on her head confining untidy grey hair.

In her still thick accent she said, 'You want a good stone? Pale stone? I found stone for you. Come.'

She hunched down the steps, went to the back of the battered little truck standing on the gravel, and lifted a piece of tattered canvas.

It was a big stone, bigger than Alex would need, probably. Matty turned it over, straining for leverage on the ridged, orange-brown crust, and it thumped on to the tray of the truck, exposing a side where the crust was thinner and a faint gleam of pale green showed through.

'I won't know until I cut it, Matty,' Alex said, but already anticipation was stirring within. This time, perhaps, it might be the right stone.

She helped Matty carry it into the studio, and over to the large wheel. When they lifted the stone on to the cutting bench it overhung the edge of the wood, and Matty had to steady it for her as she turned on the cooling water and made the cut. It was almost big enough to need a special saw set up outside, which she didn't have because most of her work was on smaller pieces of jade.

The saw bit through smoothly with a muted,

grinding howl, and she deftly caught the falling slice before turning off the machine and easing the bulk of the stone back to survey the wet, gleaming smoothness of the cut face.

Matty, still holding its weight for her, watched her face anxiously.

'Good stone, eh?'

'Very good stone,' Alex breathed at last. 'If it's only like that all the way through.' Oh God, let it be, she prayed. Her fingers tingled with a familiar need, and she ran them gently over the cool, slippery surface of palest, translucent green. 'Where did you find it, Matty?'

'That's a secret. My secret, Alex. It's a good place for greenstone.' They eased the stone down on to the water-darkened floorboards.

'Matty,' said Alex, eyeing her, 'you haven't been poaching, have you?' If it had been found on someone else's claim, and it was as valuable as this initial cut suggested, they could both be in trouble in the event that it was discovered. A not unlikely event, considering the uncanny speed and accuracy of the Coast grapevine.

But Matty was drawing herself up indignantly. 'I don't poach, Alex! I tell you, I know all the best places, I got lots of claims of my own, you know that. Only I don't want any poaching in *my* place, see? This is good stone, *my* stone! You buy it, it's yours. No trouble, Alex. I swear on the grave of my husband.'

Matty did poach, she knew. Most people did, and the owners of claims seldom complained about small pieces of jade being collected by fossickers. But a big find was a different matter. And Matty knew that as well as she did. Alex looked at her shrewdly and decided that she wasn't stupid or inexperienced enough to think she could get away with filching a first-class stone from someone else's claim.

'I beg your pardon, Matty,' she said humbly. She doubted that Matty had 'lots of' claims; most of them belonged now to three large companies dealing in jade, but there were the odd scattered small claims about like the Terawitis'. 'Of course it's yours. And I'd like to buy it. How much?'

In spite of appearances Matty was a shrewd and hard-bargaining businesswoman, and she loved to haggle. The outrageous price she first suggested was merely a starting point.

When Alex shook her head, Matty launched into a graphic description of the difficulties and dangers of hunting for greenstone: the long trek into the mountains through the dripping, dense tree cover of beech, kahikatea and rimu, five-finger and kaikawaka; the fording of icy streams; the long days and nights alone with the mists rolling down from the rocky bluffs and up from the Tasman, and only the bellbirds, the wekas and the burble of mountain waters for company.

'Very pathetic,' said Alex, knowing that Matty loved the life and could have retired years ago if she had wanted to. 'How much do you really want?'

'Alex, you are not a hard woman. You get good money from this city joker—he's rich, eh? Big car—a real flash feller. I hear he stays at the best hotel in Hoki, eh?'

'He's a businessman, Matty, and he knows what jade is worth.'

The end price was more than she would have expected, but Matty would not come down any further. Finally Alex said, 'All right, Matty. If it's as good as it looks so far, I expect you'll get it. But I'll have to talk to Mr Lewis about it. It's a bigger piece than I really need, and he may not agree to buy it.'

She had been told to contact him when she found a suitable stone, she remembered. That evening she sat gloating alone in the studio, studying the stone, touching it and feeling the warm sweet flow of longing aching in her fingers, and the growing excitement in the pit of her stomach. She wandered about inspecting her equipment, making sure everything was ready, coming back every now and then compulsively to assure herself of the colour and hardness and promise of beauty held in the nephrite.

She sat down to write a letter to Richard Lewis, to let him know that she had bought a likely piece of jade, and that she would cut into it further in the morning and confirm it. But instinct and experience told her she was right. And something else nagged at her, too. She knew he would like to be there when she made the cut. He wanted to see the work at every stage.

She fingered the card he had given her, reading the telephone number in one corner of it. Finally she went to the telephone in the wide hallway and made a collect call to Christchurch.

She recognised his voice instantly, surprising herself. He accepted the call without question, and surprised her again by saying, when the operator's impersonal voice had clicked off the line, 'Alex?'

It was a moment before she said, 'Alex Cameron here, Mr Lewis. I thought you would like to know that I've found a piece of nephrite for the dragon.'

His voice sounded cooler as he said, 'Good. May I come and see it?'

'I'd like to cut into it a bit more as soon as possible. The prospector is waiting for a decision. And she wants a lot of money for it. It's rather bigger than I need, but I'll have to buy the whole piece.'

'If it's the right stuff, buy it. I can get a plane tomorrow. Can you wait until I come?'

Just like that, she thought. A plane and then, presumably, a taxi or hired car. 'All right,' she said, 'I'll wait.'

She was alone when he arrived in a rental car. He slammed the door, bounded up the steps and rapped on the open front door before walking into the studio as though he had every right to be there. Which he did, Alex reminded herself, pushing back her hair and rising from the stool where she had been polishing another fish-hook against the wheel. She switched off the motor and said, 'Good morning, Mr Lewis.'

A quick frown brought his dark brows together. 'The name's Richard,' he said. 'And I'm not going to call you *Ms* Cameron.'

He had called her Mrs Cameron when they first met, and then nothing until last night on the phone, when he had said, sounding pleased and surprised, 'Alex?'

She stood with her back to the bench, her hand gripping its edge. 'Everyone calls me Alex,' she admitted.

He came into the room, seeming both taller and broader than she remembered, a suede jacket slung over his shoulder, dark fitting pants contrasting with a pale green shirt that had a faint silky stripe running through it and was open at the neck. His eyes took her in and she was suddenly aware of her stance, leaning on the bench, one leg casually crossed over the other under the thin cotton of her long printed skirt; and she saw in his eyes the unconscious seductiveness of it, how the shape of her breasts became more defined under the faded tee-shirt, and the line of her thighs was emphasised, by the way she was standing.

She moved swiftly, jerking her body straight, and he smiled, standing in front of her. 'Right, Alex,' he said, 'let's see this jade, shall we?'

He threw his jacket down on the bench and followed her as she took him to the corner where the stone lay on the floor. He hunkered down and ran his hand over the crust and then smoothed the cut edge with his fingertips. 'Shall I lift it for you?' he asked her.

She smothered a ridiculous urge to tell him she could manage it on her own, and nodded.

He did it with relative ease, using his muscles the right way, rising from his haunches with the stone cradled in his arms, and she switched on the motor and started the water going, then cut through, feeling her way, keeping it carefully straight while he steadied it for her as Matty had done.

Afterwards he stood silently by as she examined the thick chunk, and when she had put it down he said, 'Okay?'

She took a deep breath, let it out in a sigh, and said, 'Yes. Perfect.'

'Then, whatever it costs, we'll pay it.'

'Your Mr Mason must have a lot of money.'

'Enough. He may not have much longer in

which to spend it. He might as well get what he wants.'

She told him to make the cheque out to Matty, and while he did it she stood with her hands roving over the stone.

'You can't wait to get started, can you?' he asked her as he put the cheque down on the bench by his jacket.

Her eyes were intent on the picture that her mind was transmitting to her hands. She glanced up at him and said simply, 'No.'

'May I watch?'

She had told him she didn't work with an audience. She looked at him, again, intending to say no, but something in his eyes made her hesitate.

He said, 'I want to stay for a while.' His voice was quiet, but there was a compelling quality in it, and in the hard gaze of his eyes. She knew that he wouldn't get in the way, wouldn't distract her with hovering or questions. She shrugged, pretending indifference, and turned away from him, running her thumb over the greenstone, turning it, almost losing control of it until he came swiftly over and silently helped her to get it lined up as she wanted.

She worked in silence, cutting a block to the size she needed, and Richard stayed well aside, only moving to her aid when she was having difficulty manoeuvring the block into position. Discarded pieces of the crust clunked to the floor, and he picked them up and carefully deposited them in the large wooden box Alex kept for scraps.

When she had a piece roughly the right size, she took it to the workbench. He shifted unobtrusively aside, only sweeping his jacket out of her way, and leaning on the wall near the door while she sat looking at the block from every side, absorbed in studying the almost indiscernible grain, the opacity and luminescence that showed at different angles. She reached for the marking pencil and the photographs of the dragon, and began making careful marks on the jade, so absorbed that she didn't notice when Richard Lewis went out, only looking up once to find him gone, and staring blankly for a moment or two at the wall where he had been lounging, before returning to her work.

She took the block to a smaller cutting wheel, and began paring off corners which she had marked, each cut carefully made, inspecting the increasingly odd shape after every one to ensure she was doing the right thing.

She put it down to study the photographs again, and a voice said, 'I've made you some lunch. Here, or in the kitchen?'

She turned, startled, and saw him in the doorway, coming towards her. 'I thought you'd gone!' she said.

'I helped myself to your kitchen, since you seemed to be too busy to think about food. Do you often forget to eat?'

She shook her head, rather bemusedly. 'What's the time?'

'Nearly two.'

'I'm sorry,' Alex said automatically. 'I didn't even offer you a cup of tea. I suppose you're starving.'

'It isn't me I'm worried about. You can't work effectively on an empty stomach. Come and get something in it, will you?'

She came reluctantly, and sat at the table, not noticing what she ate, realising only vaguely that he had made an adequate meal with whatever he had found in her fridge and cupboards. He didn't talk to her, only placed things on her plate and watched her eat them, and then poured coffee for her.

The coffee seemed to have a revivifying effect, and her eyes lost their abstracted look as she blinked and really looked at him for the first time, sitting opposite her with a coffee mug in his hand, his strange, dark amber eyes fixed on her with something like exasperation.

'Well, hello,' he said softly, recognising her return to the real world.

Alex said, 'I'm sorry. You've been very kind.'

'Oh, no. I believe in looking after the workers. You're more or less on my payroll now. Do you often go into a trance when you're working?'

'I wasn't in a trance. It's an interesting project, and takes a great deal of concentration.'

'Obviously. Do you get so interested often?'

She shook her head.

He asked, 'Would you like to?'

Alex put down her cup and smiled. 'If you're trying to make me admit that I'm glad I took this on——'

'I'm not scoring any points,' he said swiftly. 'It was just a question. Conversation.'

'You don't strike me as the sort of person to make idle conversation.'

'No, I'm not. I didn't say it was idle conversation.'

She waited for him to elaborate, but he didn't, and she decided rather irritably that she wasn't going to ask him.

She got up and started to remove the dishes and cups from the table. Richard stood, too. 'I'll do it,' he said. 'Go back to your studio, if you like. Where's Jane, by the way?'

'Celebrating the beginning of the holidays by picnicking with Shawn. They took the horses.'

She relinquished the dishes into his hands as he took them from her, but she didn't go straight away. Instead, she stayed for a few minutes watching him clear the table with quick efficiency. As he ran water into the sink, he glanced at her and said, 'Get going. I can manage here.'

She went out, and when he had finished and hung up the tea-towel he had used, he strolled back into the studio and watched as she turned the chunk of cut stone on the bench, making pencil marks, and then comparing it with the photographs spread before her.

He noticed the way her hair fell against her neck and curved softly against her cheek, until she pushed it back quickly and bent to the photographs again, holding the end of the pencil lightly between her teeth for a moment as she looked thoughtfully from one to the other.

She looked up and saw him watching her, and for a second or two their eyes met and held, before she turned away from him to study the stone again.

He came over to her and stood with his hand on the bench. 'How's it coming?' he asked quietly.

'This is only the beginning.'

'I know that,' he said with patience. 'Can you estimate how long it will take you to finish it?'

'Possibly months. I do have other things to do as well.'

'I thought I'd made it clear that we want you to concentrate on this for as long as it takes.' He was frowning, and his voice had hardened.

'I will, as much as possible,' she said, 'but I have one or two other commissions to fulfil that I'd already started on—not as complicated as this, but they'll take a little time. And I can't just stop supplying the retailers altogether. They're my bread-and-butter, after all. They'll still be here when you and your commission have ridden off into the sunset.'

'I gave you a pretty hefty deposit on this, just so that you wouldn't have to earn bread-and-butter from other firms.'

'Look, I will be cutting out other work as much as I can, but I won't let down regular clients for your sake, Mr Lewis.'

'I'm not asking you to——'

'That's what it amounts to.'

'You didn't say anything about this when you accepted the money.'

Alex slipped off the stool she had been sitting on, and stood facing him. 'All right, Mr Lewis. I didn't realise that you thought you'd bought me. Finding the right stone might have taken months. What was I supposed to do? Sit around and twiddle my thumbs while I waited for it? If you think I took your money under false pretences, you can have it back. And you can have your commission back, too. And these!'

She turned to pick up the photos, gathering them into her hand and holding them out to him.

Richard snapped, 'Don't be ridiculous!' and took them from her only to fling them down again on the bench. 'I'm not accusing you of false pretences, or anything of the sort. I thought you understood——'

'Well, I'm sorry, but I didn't. I suppose you're used to writing a cheque and telling people you expect things done yesterday, but on the Coast we don't work like that. Here you take your turn just like anyone else. You'll simply have to accept it, or take your commission elsewhere.'

His eyes glinted unpleasantly, but his voice was even. 'You know I don't want to do that. Obviously there's been a misunderstanding. Perhaps I should have got you to sign a formal contract.'

'Perhaps you should,' she said curtly. 'I'll do this as soon as I possibly can, Mr Lewis, because, quite frankly, I don't like doing business with your kind, so the sooner I'm finished the better I'll like it. But I will not force other clients to await your convenience.'

She turned away from him, expecting him to leave. But instead he stayed right where he was, his face grim as he said, 'I don't expect that, and of course I'm not taking my commission elsewhere. And would you mind explaining what you mean by "my kind"?'

She took a deep breath, clamped her lips tightly for a moment, and then said, determinedly calm, 'Nothing. I'm sorry, it wasn't meant to be personal.'

'Yes, it was. Only you've got cold feet and decided to take it back.'

She turned to him, her eyes clear and green and challenging. 'I haven't. I've just remembered my manners.'

He laughed, making her blink in doubtful surprise. Then, the laughter fading from his face, he looked at her thoughtfully. 'You think I'm some kind of arrogant fool who imagines that money can buy anything, is that it?'

'I don't think for a moment that you're a fool, Mr Lewis.'

His narrowed eyes were fixed on her face. 'Thanks. I'd like to be able to return the compliment.'

Flushing with anger, she said, 'Don't worry. I know exactly what you think of me.'

'So tell me,' he invited sarcastically.

Alex shook her head. 'Never mind. I really don't care, anyway. If you want to look down your middle-class nose at me and my clothes and my life-style, go ahead. Whatever makes you happy.'

'Where did you get the idea that I look down on you?'

'Oh, come *on*! I saw the expression on your face the very first time we met, and I don't suppose you've changed your opinion.'

'No,' he agreed coolly, 'I haven't.'

'Well then——' She lifted her shoulder carelessly, turning away from him, and he had the distinct impression that she was trying to hide hurt. He said, 'Alex——' and reached out to touch her arm, but she moved away from him towards the door, saying, 'This is a rather unbusinesslike conversation, isn't it? And pointless. I'll see you out, if you don't mind. I'd like to get on with my work.'

And she didn't want him watching it any longer, obviously. He reluctantly went after her out on to the veranda.

'Alex——' he tried again, as he joined her.

'Goodbye, Mr Lewis,' she said firmly. 'If you insist, I'll let you know when the next stage of the carving is completed. It may not be for several weeks. Apart from the other work I have to finish first, I need to study the rough block very carefully before I make any more cuts. They have to be just right. I'm sure you appreciate *that*.'

'Yes, of course,' he said impatiently. 'Take as much time as you need.'

'I will.' She stood with her hand on the veranda post by the steps, and waited for him to go, her expression shuttered, her eyes fixed on his shirt.

'You don't have any idea what I thought that first day,' he said. 'You were looking at *me* as though I was something the cat dragged in, anyway. That annoyed me, I admit. It didn't stop me thinking you were a very attractive woman.'

He stepped closer to her as her eyes met his in surprise. But the surprise was immediately superseded by wariness, and if anything her expression became more wooden. 'It's all right, Mr Lewis,' she said. 'You don't need to try and soothe my feelings, I'm not particularly bothered by your low opinion of me.'

He looked at her with exasperation and said, 'You *are* a fool, Alex Cameron.' Unexpectedly his hand shot out to grasp her shoulders and pull her up against him. Her head whipped back in shock, and he bent swiftly to kiss her mouth, the pressure of his lips brief and hard against the startled softness of hers.

'And the name is Richard,' he said as he released her abruptly, before taking the steps in two strides and slamming himself into the car.

CHAPTER FOUR

RICHARD drove to Hokitika with the taste of her lips on his, a keenly pleasurable memory that stayed with him for a long time afterwards.

And Alex walked back into the house with her fingers at her mouth, at first tentatively, then fiercely rubbing at it, wiping away the sensation of the man's mouth on hers, blotting out the memory of firm hands on her shoulders, the faint tangy scent of clean masculine skin, the hardness of his chest against her breasts.

Christmas came and went quietly, Alex and Jane spending it with the Terawitis, absorbed into the informal warmth of their family celebrations. A card had arrived on Christmas Eve from Richard, printed with the name of the firm, butt inscribed 'With my best wishes, Alex and Jane, from Richard Lewis.'

In the next few weeks Alex finished carving and polishing a *mere*, the ceremonial hand-weapon of chiefs, for a Maori client, and a necklace set in a delicate gold setting for a man who had wanted something unique and beautiful for his wife to mark their fiftieth wedding anniversary. And she polished and set a number of cabuchons for jewellery which she could supply to her regular retail outlets at intervals.

And every day she looked at the photographs of the dragon, and at the block of jade that sat beside them, the rough cuts milky-green and dull, in its dry state. Each day she saw more clearly just how it must be cut and shaped to duplicate the original in the photographs.

When finally she was ready to work on it again, she went into the studio and spent several minutes just turning the stone in her hands, examining it and getting the feel of its weight and texture fixed in her mind and her fingers.

Then, with one of the smaller saws, she made some careful cuts in the surface until she could see the rough shape of the little dragon emerging in a crude, squared-off form. The trickle of water cooling the diamond edge gave back the jade's translucent beauty, and she began to feel a sense of pleasurable expectancy as she held it up to the light and admired it.

She had not contacted Richard Lewis again, but that night he phoned and asked her how the work was progressing.

She asked, 'Are you clairvoyant, Mr Lewis?'

'I'm not clairvoyant, and I'm not *Mr* Lewis,' he said. 'I thought I'd made that rather clear.'

She hadn't thought he would bring that up. The kiss had been a half-angry impulse, surely, something quite out of character. She would have expected him to regret it almost immediately, and not refer to it again.

She didn't answer, and after a moment he asked, 'Have you got any further with the dragon?'

'A very little. I just began working on it today.'

'Does that mean you've finished your other commissions?'

'Yes.'

'Then please don't take on any more until you've completed this.'

Alex was silent again, and he said, with

resignation in his voice, 'Are you counting to ten?'

She couldn't help a small laugh, but she said vexedly, 'You do have that effect on me.'

There was another pause, and then Richard said deliberately, 'Funny—you have quite a different effect on *me*.'

'Oh, I don't think it's so very different,' she said dryly before she could stop herself. She closed her eyes, cursing herself, and biting her tongue.

'You're very brave at the other end of the telephone,' he said. 'I'll see you tomorrow.'

Before she could protest or retract anything, he had hung up. *Stupid*, Alex told herself. He wanted to play games, and she had practically encouraged him with that idiotic remark. She should have just ignored his hint, pretended she didn't know what he was talking about. She wasn't in the running for games of any sort. She would have to make that very clear, next time he came. Tomorrow, he had said. Well, she would be ready for him.

It was Saturday again, and Richard phoned from Hokitika, saying he was lunching with someone, and would it be all right if he came in the afternoon?

Alex said yes, tempted to put him off, but realising that it would only be postponing the inevitable. He wasn't about to turn around and go all the way back to Christchurch without seeing her.

After an early lunch, Alex and Jane had been working on the engine of the VW, finally giving up when Alex realised that the trouble she had experienced with it the day before on her way back from a shopping trip was probably due to an electrical fault, and beyond her basic knowledge of motor mechanics. The car still stood just outside the garage, the tools they had been using lying beside it, and the two of them were sitting on the steps, while Alex tried to cheer up a glum Jane, when Richard Lewis arrived in a hired car.

Alex hadn't expected him so soon, though when she glanced at her watch she realised they had spent longer working on the engine than she had thought. Her hands were grease-streaked and her jeans dusty, and her hair was tied back with a crumpled bit of Christmas ribbon.

She got up slowly as he left his car, and he nodded to her and turned curious eyes to Jane, a dejected figure, still sitting on the steps with her chin in her hands. 'What's the trouble?' he asked.

'Say hello to Mr Lewis, Jane,' Alex chided, and the child stood up and gave him an unsmiling, 'Hello.'

Richard raised enquiring eyes to Alex, and she said, 'Our car won't go. We've been trying to fix it, but I'm afraid it's beyond me. I'll ask Paddy to look at it when he has time—he used to be a mechanic, among other things.'

'And we're supposed to go to the Glaciers tomorrow,' Jane explained. 'It was all arranged, and Shawn was coming, too.' She looked hopefully at him. 'Do you know much about cars, Mr Lewis?'

'Not a lot, I'm afraid,' he said. 'But I could take you to the Glaciers, if you like.'

'*Could* you?' Jane's face was transformed, a grin spreading across it instantaneously.

'No,' Alex said quickly. 'We can't impose on Mr Lewis——'

'You're not imposing,' he said. 'I'd like to see the Glaciers, and I don't have to be back until Monday morning. Let me take you.'

She opened her mouth to protest again, saw that he was looking at her with a challenge in his eyes, and heard Jane's disappointed, 'Oh, Mum, *please*, can't we?'

She hesitated, said to Jane, 'I'll think about it while I talk to Mr Lewis. Would you mind clearing up the tools and putting them away, darling? And then you'd better wash your hands before you do anything else.'

'I've got to do my homework, *if* we're going out tomorrow,' Jane said meaningly.

'Well, you can do it in any case,' Alex told her firmly. 'It's got to be done some time this weekend, and it might as well be now.'

'Okay.' Jane moved disconsolately over to the tools spread on a cloth on the ground, and Alex said, 'Please come in, Mr Lewis.'

She took him into the sitting room and excused herself to go and wash her hands. Looking in the mirror, she saw crossly that she had a streak of black car oil across her cheek, too, and on impulse she stripped off, had a lightning-fast shower and wrapped a towel about her to pad into the bedroom and look for a change of clothing.

She pulled on a black tee-shirt and wrapped one of her long printed skirts about her waist, hurriedly brushed out her hair, and returned to the sitting room to find Richard looking at the carvings in the cabinet.

He looked round at her and smiled. 'I've put your vase in pride of place in my bedroom,' he told her. 'Every morning when I wake, it's the first thing I see.'

She didn't want to know that. She didn't want to picture him waking and looking at the vase she had made. 'It isn't my vase, it's yours,' she said. 'You paid for it.'

Not liking the quick, hard glance he threw at her, she added at random, 'Most people put things like that in their living rooms.'

'I bought it to enjoy it myself, not to show off to other people.'

Looking at him thoughtfully, she asked, 'Don't you enjoy sharing your possessions with your friends?'

'My special friends get invited into the bedroom.'

Her lip curled, and he made a small, mock-chiding sound. 'Now, Alex, don't look like that. What a nasty mind you have!'

Annoyed, she felt herself flushing. 'You can't read my mind,' she said shortly.

'Can't I?' he challenged her softly, and she lifted her chin, giving him a hostile stare.

'Why are you so determined not to like me, Alex?' he asked her.

'You're imagining things, Mr Lewis.'

'Richard. And I'm not imagining things at all. Have you sworn off men, is that it?'

'Yes, I have. Shall we go through to the studio?'

'No, not yet. Why have you?'

'It's really none of your business, is it?' She turned away from him to cross the passageway into the studio.

He followed her, but as they entered the other room he shut the door behind them, and she looked around in wary surprise.

Smiling faintly, he said, 'I'm not going to leap on you. But if we're going to continue this conversation, I don't suppose you want Jane to hear.'

'We're not going to continue it, so you might as well open the door, Mr Lewis.' Ignoring the angry glint in his eyes, Alex turned away from him. 'Now, about the commission you gave me——'

'The hell with the commission!' he said with quiet violence. 'I want to talk about you.'

She turned to look at him again, her eyes filled with resentment. 'That's very flattering of you, I'm sure. But *I don't want to.*'

'Tell me about Jane's father,' he said. 'Is that why you don't want anything to do with men?'

She looked at him angrily, saw that he stood just inside the closed door, and guessed that if she made to leave the room he wouldn't let her. Her mouth tight, she whirled away from him and went to stand, her back rigid, looking out of one of the long up-and-down windows.

There was a lengthy silence, and at last he said quietly, 'All right, you're not going to tell me anything. I suppose I don't have any right to ask. But for God's sake stop calling me Mr Lewis. If I hear it once more from you, I won't be responsible!'

Alex turned slowly and looked at him. 'I'll show you the dragon,' she said. 'That's what you came for, isn't it?'

He didn't answer, but came away from the door to join her at the bench, and she picked up the crudely-shaped jade and let him compare it with the photographs, and explained how the next step would be to use tiny chisels and her drills for some more fine, judicious cutting to shape the limbs, the ridge of the tail, the open mouth and the eyes.

He took it in his hands, listening, and then put it carefully down. 'Will it take you long?'

'Each stage takes longer than the last. The work gets finer and more fiddly as I go along.'

She was turning away from him as he said abruptly, 'Will you let me drive you tomorrow?'

'I don't think so——'

'Why not? I'm free, and it's a shame to disappoint Jane.'

He saw the flash of temper in her eyes as she said, 'Well, I'm sorry about that, but she'll just have to be disappointed.'

Impatiently he said, 'No! That's just the point. She doesn't *have* to be disappointed, does she? Just because for some reason you're scared stiff to let me anywhere near you! What could happen to you, on a trip with two kids to chaperone us? What do you think I'd be likely to do to you, even if they weren't coming along? And what's the point of cutting off Jane's nose to spite *your* face?'

'I am not doing anything of the sort! You're not the first man to try it, you know—I won't have Jane used as a lever to put me under an obligation to you!'

Richard was astounded. 'For heaven's sake! Is that what you think I'm trying to do?'

'I told you,' she said wearily, 'it's been done before. And don't tell me your motives are different. You think because I'm a single mother I must be—available, with a little bit of persuasion. And if you're kind to my daughter,

I'll be grateful, and gratitude is such a powerful aphrodisiac, isn't it? I'm not scared of you—I'm sure you're a very civilised man, and no doubt you make love just beautifully, but go and find someone else, will you, please? I'm not interested, and there are plenty of other fish in the sea for a man with your obvious charms.'

She was going to the door when he stopped her with a hand on her arm. She tried to pull away, but he tightened his fingers and forced her round to face him. 'Alex!' he said, his face grim. 'Listen to me!'

She lifted a fist to hit at his arm, and he winced and caught her other arm, too, saying, 'You can't just hurl accusations like that and then walk away. You'll damn well *listen* to me!'

Alex stopped struggling and said, 'Let me go, then.'

Richard released her, watching her face as he said, 'I suppose I should have checked with you before I said in front of Jane that I'd drive you to the Glaciers. And I admit that my motives weren't entirely pure, either. I probably wouldn't have offered to take the children without you. Maybe that was manipulative, and I don't blame you for not liking it. But I honestly didn't think of it that way. I like Jane very much, she's a good kid. And I like you—I find you attractive and I'd hoped to get to know you better. But that doesn't mean I see you as a cheap and convenient means of sexual satisfaction. That isn't my way. I'm not responsible for what other men have done to you, and I won't be tarred with the same brush!'

Her face was stony, and he gave a short, exasperated sound and went on more forcefully,

'You seem to be convinced that you know all about me—well, you don't, lady. Not by a long chalk. Stop looking at me as Man, with a capital M, will you? I'm *a* man, Richard Lewis, Richard to you. And you're a woman, to me. Not any woman—Alex. You're Alex and you're special, and if I want you, it's because you're Alex, not because you're supposedly "available" or because it's somehow convenient for me to want you, or because single mothers are fair game.'

'*Do* you want me?'

She wasn't looking at him, but down at her hands held in front of her, one thumb rubbing the other shiny thumbnail. He stood staring at her bent head for several seconds before he said simply, 'Yes.'

When she looked up at last, he saw the rejection in her eyes, in the firm set of her mouth. 'I'm sorry,' she said. 'I'm not interested.'

He looked baffled, and the tension between them suddenly increased. He made a slight movement, and even as he checked it she stepped back from him.

A brief flare of anger showed in his eyes, but he said quietly, 'I'm sorry, too. But I'd still like to see the Glaciers, and I'd still like to take you and Jane and her friend.'

'Look, you don't have to——'

'Alex!' he interrupted. 'I very seldom do anything I don't want to. We both know where we stand now. Why make a production out of a simple invitation?'

She felt that there was more to it than that, but he had deliberately defused the tension, and his calm reasoning was making her doubts seem ridiculous. Reluctantly she said, 'Well, if you really want to——'

'I told you, I do,' he said firmly. 'I'll pick you up in the morning, and young whatshisname, too.'

'Shawn. I'll get him to come here, if you like.'

'No, we can fetch him after I've collected you two.'

'It's very kind of you——'

'I'm not being kind,' Richard said rather roughly. 'And I don't want any gratitude, thanks. Actually, I don't find it in the least aphrodisiacal.'

Alex flushed slightly, turning away to open the door, and this time he didn't try to stop her. When he followed her out to the passageway, she hesitated for a moment and then asked, 'Would you like a cup of tea? Or coffee?'

'Thank you. I thought you'd never ask.'

Her indignant eyes met a teasing, quizzical look in his, and she reluctantly smiled, shaking her head a little. 'Sit down,' she said, indicating the sitting room. 'I'll go and make it—which is it?'

'Coffee, thanks. And I'd rather come and have it in the kitchen.'

Alex shrugged. 'Please yourself.'

Richard half-sat against the table while she got out the cups and switched on the electric jug. She buttered some crackers, laying sliced cheese on top, and dusted them with black pepper from a wooden grinder.

'May I see?' he asked as she made to put the grinder down.

Alex handed it to him, and he ran his fingers over the turned wood, admiring the grain and the smooth texture. He shook some pepper grains into his palm, and sniffed at them cautiously as he placed the grinder on the table. 'Mmm,' he murmured.

Watching him, Alex laughed. 'Are you a gourmet?'

'No, I don't think so. I like food—who doesn't? But I don't claim to be any expert.'

She said, 'I'll bet you like properly ground and percolated coffee, don't you?'

'How did you guess?'

'I'm psychic,' she said lightly. It hadn't been a difficult guess. She herself liked to feel and smell things, and she knew from watching him that he appreciated sensuous experiences. Like the tang of freshly ground pepper, the feel of turned, oiled wood, the pungent aroma of percolating coffee beans, the smooth surface of polished jade. She said, 'You're not in a hurry, are you?' and put back the jar of instant coffee she had taken from the cupboard, lifting down instead a packet of coffee beans. 'Here,' she said. 'You can grind them.'

She showed him the Delft china coffee mill attached to the wall, and he put the beans in and turned the handle until the drawer underneath was filled with coarse grounds. She tipped them into the percolater, and soon the room was filled with the delicious smell of coffee while they talked about current news events, cautiously impersonal. When the coffee was ready Alex served it with a dollop of cream on top of each cup, and sprinkled cinnamon over it.

'Fantastic,' Richard murmured as he sat down at the table and took the cup from her. 'You'd have no trouble at all finding your way to a man's heart.'

She said nothing, stirring cream into her coffee, her eyes lowered. The silence lengthened.

Richard said, 'Was that the wrong thing to say?'

She looked up, smiling. 'Of course not. It was just an idle remark, wasn't it?'

She didn't expect a reply, and he made none. But her smile had been polite rather than warm, and he knew that the barrier he had started to breach was up again.

Suppressing his irritation, he asked, 'Have you always lived on the Coast?'

'I was brought up here, though I was actually born in Wellington. My father got transferred to Greymouth when I was four. He and Mum got "Coast Fever", like a lot of others who've come for a while and found they couldn't bear to live anywhere else. They stayed for the rest of their lives.'

'They died?'

'Yes. Just a few years ago.'

'I'm sorry. You've never been away again?'

'When Jane was born, I "went up North for a while"—you know? To an aunt in Auckland. Well, nine years ago it wasn't quite so— acceptable as now. Not here, anyway. Coasters are the best people in the world, but they tend to be a bit behind the times.'

He'd thought Jane was older than that. She must be tall for her age. 'So why did you come back?' he asked.

'I belong here.'

He looked at her curiously, sceptical of the affirmation in her voice.

'You don't understand, do you?' she asked.

Richard shook his head, and she said, 'It's

something that gets in your blood. The Coast is so wild and so varied. And so beautiful. The Tasman out there, thundering up on to that long, long shore, and the bluffs—you know? Those great grey stone bluffs rearing up into the sky, miles long, and the bush growing on top and below them, into the valleys and up to the mountains. The bush is so thick and green and secret, and yet when you go into it, the bellbirds are calling to each other, and the other birds, and you come on some unexpected waterfall, or a stream of clear, cold water—each one will give you a different colour of stone, not just greenstone, but all kinds of stone—pink, sometimes, or purple, and of course there's red jasper—and occasionally gold. Real gold. And it's so quiet. You can hear yourself thinking, in the bush.'

'There's no bush on the glaciers.'

'No, they're different, of course. But beautiful, too, in their own way. Majestic is the word, I suppose. You'll see for yourself tomorrow. Or have you been there before?'

'As a child. I don't remember much.'

'You'll love them. And the lakes. There are several lakes on the way.'

'You have a lot of rain, here.'

'Without it, we wouldn't have our lakes, or streams, or rainforest. Anyway, there are compensations. You should be here in winter.'

'Should I?'

'It's the best, in some ways. You get these hard, cold frosts in the mornings, and then a simply gorgeous day, still and fresh, and so sharp it could cut you. It's—indescribable. It's the Coast.'

'You're proud of being a Coaster, aren't you?' remarked Richard.

'Yes.'

'Stubborn, independent, a law unto themselves?'

Alex smiled. 'You've been listening to stories.'

'Aren't they true?'

Alex laughed. 'Probably. And then some.'

'We do know about you,' he said, 'on the other side of the mountains.' He laughed, too, and Alex asked, 'What?'

'Stories. Like the landlady who was serving beer on Sunday, and when the police raided the place, they found all her clients on their knees saying the Rosary, although the local cops knew as well as anyone that half of them were Protestants and atheists.'

Alex laughed. 'I know that one, too. They swear it's true, round here. The Coast has always thrown up characters and quick wits.'

'There's a facsimile on the wall of the bar in my hotel, of a notice that's supposed to have been put up in his office by some Victorian mining rights registrar. It says, *For the satisfaction of persons who are unwilling to take off their hats in this office, it is hereby notified that none but gentlemen are expected to do so——*'

'I bet it worked beautifully on the miners!' Alex giggled.

'I'm sure it did. I might say I've heard some pretty tall tales in that bar, especially about the West Coast ingenuity in outwitting the constabularly. Not a very law-abiding lot, are you?'

'Of course we are. We make up our own laws and obey them to the letter,' said Alex, tongue in cheek. 'Anyway, the rest of New Zealand finally got around to adopting our more civilised drinking hours, didn't they? I don't think the constabulary has needed outwitting nearly so often since six o'clock closing in the pubs was replaced by ten o'clock.' Her eyes glowed with laughter, and his smiled, too.

'There are rumours that even ten o'clock closing hasn't satisfied some diehards.'

'Surely you don't listen to rumour, Mr Lewis?'

'I beg your pardon?' he drawled.

Alex looked at him, bit her lip, and said almost meekly, 'Richard.'

He gave her an ironic little bow. 'Thank you. Maybe next time it will come easier.'

She pushed away her cup and got up. 'More coffee?'

He leaned back a little in his chair and looked at her. 'No, thanks. I have a feeling I've outstayed my welcome.'

'Not at all,' she said, but there was no warmth in her voice, and she didn't urge him to stay. His smile was a little grim as he got up to go.

CHAPTER FIVE

THE day was fine and cool the next morning, but as they reached the first of the lakes on their way south the sunlight pushed its way through the stark trees bordering the water, and shimmered on its surface, with a promise of warmth to come.

The rimu, rata and beech kept the sun from reaching them as they followed the road through the bush, but each time they lost the trees the blaze on the windscreen grew stronger, and when they stopped at the township of Franz Josef to buy a snack and drinks, they found it was basking in summer.

They made a further short stop at the little church of St James just out of the township, its famous picture window framing a magnificent view of the glacier which gave the town its name. Jane stopped to read the plaque explaining how the minister had dreamed of a church built of local stone, overlooking the glacier, but had been persuaded by his bishop to build in wood.

'I think stone would have been nicer,' she said. Richard smiled and agreed with her. They seemed to get on very well. Shawn, too, apparently liked Richard. He treated the children as intelligent human beings, and didn't talk down to them. Alex liked that. Wearing casual clothes, and in a relaxed mood, he was very attractive. She felt herself growing wary, answering his remarks on the scenery and the day briefly, her smiles stiff.

He cast her a wry glance as they turned down the road to the glacier, and from then on concentrated on his driving. The road became increasingly rough, and the vegetation scanty. The children began reading out the little signs that detailed the glacier's position in former times, testifying to the rate at which it was receding.

Across the grey expanse of shingle they saw a tour bus and a couple of cars at the foot of the steep incline where the glacier nestled high in a cleft, the pale sky behind it, and Jane and Shawn leaned over from the back seat so as not to miss anything.

When they reached the car-park and got out the chill off the ice was noticeable, and they all donned warm parkas and boots for the climb ahead of them.

The ice was blue and jagged, and deceptively far away. Each time they crested another smooth-worn, lichen-dusted rock outcrop, with the help of cut steps and a sturdy wooden railing, another seemingly identical one remained to be sur-mounted. But at last, panting, they reached the glacier and were able to touch the edge of it, although it was too dangerous to walk on.

Jane and Shawn fossicked a few lumps of dirtied ice, threatening each other with pieces down the backs of their clothes, and then sat on a rock side by side, just gazing at the dazzling tumble of ice boulders and pinnacles.

The climb had made them quite warm, but the icy air had chilled Alex's nose, and she rubbed it ruefully with a gloved hand. Richard was watching her, and she said, 'It's pretty cold.'

'I'd noticed.' His tone was ironic, and she

shifted her eyes hastily from his to admire the
glacier again.

'Had enough?' he asked the children, and they
jumped up, ready to start the descent.

Richard offered his hand to Alex, but she
pretended not to notice, negotiating the curving,
downward path without help.

At Fox, the glacier was closer to the road, and
as they drove between high, intimidating bluffs of
bare grey stone, a shallow river of grey-blue ran
swiftly beside them. Nearer the source, huge
blocks of ice littered the shores, and the children
were able to go down and retrieve a couple of
smaller chunks to exclaim over and show to the
two adults. The end of the glacier was nearby,
blue pillars of ice standing starkly as though
holding it back, and the river flowed from its
melting ice-fall.

They picnicked later at a spot on a side road
that gave a magnificent view of the ice edging its
way between two peaks in its slow journey to sea-
level. The children were more interested in food
by this time, but when she had packed up the
remainders and poured herself and Richard
coffee from a flask, Alex took her cup and went to
stand where the trees framed the distant prospect
like a postcard picture.

Richard came and joined her, and for a few
minutes they stood silently looking and sipping
their coffee.

'The kids are enjoying it,' he said.

'Yes.'

He waited, and then said deliberately, 'But you
seem bored.'

'Of course I'm not bored,' she denied quickly.
'I'm not a very talkative person.'

'Rot. You talk when you want to. You just don't want to talk to me, at the moment. I'd like to know why.'

'You're imagining things, Mr Lewis.'

She heard the quick sucking in of his breath, as though he wanted to say something explosive. Then he downed the rest of his coffee and flung away the dregs with a movement so violent that she flinched, but he only turned from her abruptly and left her standing alone while he went to the car and opened up the boot ready for the picnic things.

He stood about looking impatient, and Alex hurriedly finished her coffee and stowed the cups away. Within five minutes they were on their way again, and while Jane and Shawn played word games and sang in the back, the two adults sat in stony silence.

It couldn't last, of course. Eventually Alex was drawn into a discussion with Jane and Shawn about the probable number of years left before the glaciers melted away altogether, and Richard chipped in with a calculation based on the miles per year that the ice had already receded. Alex challenged his figures, and when he insisted on sticking to them, she took out a notebook and pencil and began writing down her version and his.

'There you are,' she said as she showed them to him. 'Admit that you must be wrong!'

He glanced at the page she had thrust in front of him and said, 'I admit nothing. You haven't taken into account the different rate of melting as the glacier grows smaller. It's all a matter of relativity.'

'That's an incalculable variable,' Alex said crushingly.

'What does that mean?' Jane demanded curiously, leaning over Alex's shoulder.

Richard threw her a grin and said, 'It means your mother's beaten in the argument and she's using big words to try and confuse the opposition.'

Jane giggled, and Alex said, 'And that, Richard, is sophistry.'

'What's sophistry?' Jane turned to Alex.

'What people use when they can't think of a logical, reasonable answer to an argument.'

'It's a handy label,' Richard said, 'used by those who prefer personal insults to logical, reasonable arguments.'

Jane rolled her eyes and, saying, 'I give up!' bounced back on to her seat, and Richard shot a provocative look at Alex and murmured, 'But I forgive you.'

She was caught between laughter and indignation, and when she saw the slight crease at the corner of his mouth as he returned his attention to the road, the laughter won. She had been forgiven for that 'Mr' earlier, and she was glad.

Stopping at Lake Ianthe, they were surprised to see a white heron stalking along the water's edge among the reeds.

'It's rare, isn't it?' Richard asked quietly, and Jane said, 'We've seen them before, haven't we, Shawn? But not very often. Lots of people go to the sanctuary at Okarito to see them, but you have to have special permission, and you're supposed to be an ornithologist or something to get it. He's a beauty, isn't he?'

Alex wasn't listening, her attention caught by the bird with its long legs and beak and graceful neck, the lake reflecting a greenish tinge on to its white plumage. For several minutes it stayed poised and still by the water. Alex, her gaze alert and concentrated, tried to imprint the shape of it on her mind.

At last it took off, it's wings flapping three or four times and lifting it into the shimmering air, then lazily moving until it disappeared into the trees.

Alex realised that Richard was looking at her, his eyes intent and curious. As hers met them, he said, 'You'll finish the dragon first, won't you?'

How had he known that she meant to carve the heron? Her face registered surprise, and he smiled and said, 'You had that look. I've learned to recognise it.'

'Top of the class,' she murmured, but there was no sting in the sarcasm. She felt disturbed by his perception. It wasn't welcome.

Back in the car, she began thinking of a stone to use for the heron. Some nephrites came in milky white shades, with just the merest hint of green. She would keep a watch out for a good piece, not too large.

When they arrived at Shawn's house, it was getting dark. Charlotte Terawiti, Shawn's mother, made them come in, and insisted they stay to eat a meal. Alex cast a sideways glance at Richard, wondering how he would fit in with the large noisy family in the rambling old house with its cosy, shabby furniture. She was suprised at how well he did, sitting at the long scarred table between two of Shawn's older brothers and asking their father questions about farming practice, admitting his ignorance without embarrassment, and apparently showing a genuine interest in learning something new. He tackled the huge plate of wild pork and vegetables set before him by his hostess with obvious relish, and Alex, served with vegetables alone, thought that possibly he was glad not to have to put up with meatless fare again.

After the dishes were disposed of, they sat in the lounge and the visitor was regaled with tall stories from the history of the Coast.

Eruera, the oldest son, who had been sitting next to Richard throughout dinner, set the ball rolling with the tale of a public official whose duties made him unpopular, who was inveigled into a pub on New Year's Eve on the pretext of showing goodwill. While someone bought him drinks several other men went outside to where he had left his horse and cart, unharnessed the horse, pushed the shafts of the cart through the palings of a fence, and harnessed the horse up again on the other side of the fence.

The Terawitis must have all heard the story many times, but the whole family roared as Eruera described the official's puzzled reactions when he came to collect his transport.

Encouraged by this success, Eruera embarked on another tale, about a mare famous for her speed who had interrupted the Greymouth races to have a foal on the track, but then gallantly got up and finished the race, only to be beaten by a nose—by the foal.

Another brother followed with the story of the publican who told suspicious police that the fifteen men drinking in his bar on Sunday were all private guests of the family—and to prove it sat the 'guests' around his table for a Sunday dinner consisting of one very modest roast with accompanying vegetables, obviously designed to feed no more than himself, his wife and their two small children.

From then on the stories flowed thick and fast, and Alex reflected, watching Richard's somewhat bemused appreciation of them, that the Terawitis had inherited the traditional raconteurs' skill of the West Coasters, through both the Irish and the Maori sides of the family. Albert, Shawn's father, told how some of his Maori ancestors who had helped crew a whaling ship to California during the gold-rush days had been unimpressed by the yellow stuff that got the white men so excited. 'There's plenty of that back home,' they said scornfully. And there was, but it was a few more years before the West Coast and Otago gold-rushes began in their homeland.

Richard laughed, and said, 'But they had a proper respect for greenstone, anyway.'

'Of course,' Albert agreed. 'It was hard, and useful for tools.'

'And beautiful,' Alex put in. 'Don't tell me the early Maoris didn't realise that too.'

'Oh, they did,' Albert agreed, '. . . . later. But at first it was its purely functional qualities that made the stuff so precious.'

'And its rarity,' Alex murmured.

'That's true. Yes, there was a good deal of blood spilt for greenstone in those days.' Albert turned to Richard. 'Did you know it was for the greenstone that Te Rauparaha came south in the 1820's?'

'No,' Richard admitted. 'I thought the old warrior just had a power complex. He must have been quite a general, in his day.'

'A highly intelligent man,' Albert said. 'Of course he had guns, lots of guns, before most of the other tribes were properly armed, which gave him a terrific advantage. But also he knew how to organise a military campaign. I have an admiration for him.' He grinned, looking over at Alex. 'Alex doesn't agree with me. To her he was a bloodthirsty old warmonger. She doesn't approve of him.'

Richard said, 'Alex and I have already discussed her views on warfare. She believes in passive resistance.'

His eyes met hers for a few moments, his smile a gentle taunt. Alex looked away as Albert laughed and said, 'I don't think that would have worked with Te Rauparaha. She would have ended up in one of his ovens!'

Alex grimaced at him, and looked over to where Jane was curled up in a deep armchair, her head drooping. 'I think it's time my daughter was in bed,' she said. 'Could we go, Richard?'

'Of course.' He was on his feet at once, shaking hands with Albert and thanking Charlotte for the meal. Jane stood up sleepily and, once installed in the car, leaned her head into the corner of the rear seat and was already asleep when they reached Alex's house. Richard said, 'Don't disturb her, I'll carry her.'

Alex started to protest, but he was out of the car and had lifted Jane into his arms in seconds. She led the way inside to Jane's bedroom, and he placed the sleepily murmuring child on the bed, then stood by as Alex removed shoes and socks, and quietly went out when she started unzipping and unbuttoning the child's clothes.

He was lounging in the doorway of the sitting room when she came out into the passageway, and she stopped, feeling suddenly awkward, not knowing how to get rid of him without seeming rude.

He waited, his hands pushed into his pockets, his legs crossed. Alex moved slowly towards him, saying formally, 'Thank you very much for the day. We both enjoyed it.'

He still didn't move, his eyes unreadable as they rested on her face.

'And thanks for bringing Jane inside,' she added. She couldn't drag her eyes away from his, and that was stupid. There was a strong pull of attraction about him; she felt it and hoped that he didn't realise how he affected her. She tried to think of something more to say, some gracious way of telling him to go. She stood there for a few seconds, then said jerkily, 'Well, I suppose we'll be seeing you again some time. I'll let you know when there's anything more to see—with the dragon.'

'Oh, shut up,' he drawled suddenly, and although he stayed propped against the door frame, his arm snaked out about her waist and pulled her up against him.

It was so unexpected that she found herself going fluidly with the movement, her body curving along the length of his as he brought her close, her mouth softening under his kiss, parting for him when he exerted a slight, demanding pressure.

The pleasure of it was a sweet shock, and for a long, drowning moment she simply gave herself up to it, mindlessly enjoying the taste of his lips, the confident strength of the arms that held her waist, and the contrast of his hard masculinity and her feminine pliancy.

When her brain took over and she tried to draw

away, he ignored her silent protest at first, his lips still moving over hers with sensual satisfaction, and his arms tightening fractionally to negate her resistance.

She pushed strongly against his chest, and he lifted his head, looking at her with narrowed eyes, then releasing her quite slowly.

He straightened away from the doorway, and Alex, trying to keep her voice cool and steady, said, 'Thank you again. You've had your payment. Now please go.'

She turned to the front door and pulled it wide for him, not looking at his face. For a second or so she thought he was not going, because he hadn't moved. When he did he came and stood in front of her, and his voice was biting as he said, 'That was a cheap and nasty crack, Alex, and not worthy of you.'

She felt herself flushing, and her hand tightened on the door knob. He was entitled to be angry. He had kissed her because he had seen the way she was looking at him, and he had had every reason to think that it would be welcome. She hadn't even attempted to stop him at first, and he wasn't stupid. He knew damned well that the attraction between them was mutual.

In a low voice, she said, 'Yes, you're right. I'm sorry.'

'I don't want to rush you,' he said. 'But you kissed me back, just then, for a little while. Why have you gone all defensive about it?'

Alex shook her head. 'Let's just skip the post-mortem, shall we? It won't happen again, I promise you.'

Startled at her grim tone, and a little piqued, he said, 'You want to bet?'

She looked up at him, her green eyes determined. 'Don't!'

Richard frowned. 'Just tell me why.'

'Look, I don't have to tell you a thing,' she snapped, 'but if you really want to know, I'm in no need of a man. I know that's hard to believe, but I really don't need anyone. I'm fine, just fine, on my own, and that's how I intend to stay. No strings, no affairs, no man in my life. Okay, so I kissed you back. It's been a long time since— well, since. Anyway, it was very pleasant, your technique is faultless, but I don't want any repeat performances, thanks. Is that clear?'

'No. You still haven't told me why. All right,' he said, as she looked away from him, her mouth tight. 'All right, I'm going away. I won't bother you any more tonight. But I'll be back, Alex. And I'll keep coming.'

'You'll be wasting your time,' she said coldly.

And Richard, his hand itching to reach out and close around her bent head to make her meet his kiss, controlled the urge with an effort and said, with a confidence born of the elation that her brief but unmistakable response had wakened in him, 'I don't think so.'

His thoughts on the way back to his hotel were all of Alex. Her softness and the almost submissive way she had moved into his arms had surprised him. She was so tall for a woman, and he had noticed before the strength of her long-fingered hands, the ease with which she lifted quite heavy lumps of stone, the lithe way she moved. He had not expected the sudden yielding of her mouth, her body, to his touch, or the supple arching of her back against his encircling arm, which had given him a fierce pleasure. He very much wanted to experience it again, and to give Alex pleasure, too. She had admitted, tacitly, that she had enjoyed the kiss. Richard set his jaw. He wasn't going to allow her to back off. They could be so good together, he knew it. She was afraid, afraid of something—seeming easy, perhaps. Or of being hurt. He didn't think she was easy, and he didn't want to hurt her. But he wanted very much to know her—in every sense. He wanted to explore her personality, find out all about her. He wondered again about Jane's father. Had he been as young as she must have been? Or an older man, taking advantage of a teenager? That thought brought with it a savage, contemputous anger.

His hands tightened on the wheel, so that he had to consciously relax them, laughing at himself. Alex had made it clear that none of this was any of his business, anyway. But she would tell him, all the same. Some day. He would see to it. He had an absorbing curiosity about her that he could not remember experiencing with any other woman. There had been several women in his life, but he had never wanted or needed to know about their past lovers, their lives before they met him. It had been enough to know that at the moment they interested, and were interested in, him.

Alex was different. He wanted to know everything about her, wanted her to feel the same way about him.

He wondered how she did feel about him, was intensely curious to know what she thought of him. She had said that it had been a long time, implied that this was the reason she had at first

Introducing
Harlequin Temptation™

Have you ever thought
you were in love
with one man...only
to feel attracted to another?

That's just one of the temptations you'll find facing the women in new *Harlequin Temptation* romance novels.

Sensuous...contemporary...compelling...reflecting today's love relationships!

The passionate torment of a woman torn between two loves...the siren call of a career...the magnetic advances of an impetuous employer—nothing is left unexplored in this romantic new series from Harlequin. You'll thrill to a candid new frankness as men and women seek to form lasting relationships in the face of temptations that threaten true love. Begin with your FREE copy of *First Impressions.* Mail the reply card today!

First Impressions
by Maris Soule

He was involved with her best friend.

Tracy Dexter couldn't deny her attraction to her new boss. Mark Prescott looked more like a jet set playboy than a high school principal—and he acted like one, too. It wasn't right for Tracy to go out with him, not when her friend Rose had already staked a claim. It wasn't right, even though Mark's eyes were so persuasive, his kiss so probing and intense. Even though his hands scorched her body with a teasing, raging fire...and when he gently lowered her to the floor she couldn't find the words to say no.

A word of warning to our regular readers: While Harlequin books are always in good taste, you'll find more sensuous writing in new *Harlequin Temptation* than in other Harlequin romance series.

® ™Trademarks of Harlequin Enterprises Ltd.

Get this romance novel FREE
as your introduction to new

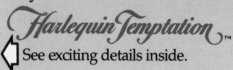

Harlequin Temptation ™

◁ See exciting details inside.

allowed him that blind, headlong response. Sexual frustration and nothing else. His confidence wavered, for a moment replaced by anger.

Deliberately he called up the memory of her mouth opening under his, of her breasts as they pressed against his chest, the tender, yearning stance of her body when he had held her.

With certainty he knew that he had not been just any man to her. That it was himself, Richard, she had been kissing, responding to. The anger died. He could make her respond again. And again. As he contemplated it, his foot unconsciously descended hard on the accelerator. The car leaped forward into the darkness.

CHAPTER SIX

THE next time he saw her, at the beginning of February, Richard knew she had deliberately closed herself off from him. Her manner was cool and brisk as she showed him the dragon and stood aside to allow him to pick it up for himself.

Richard glanced at her, his eyes hard, and examined the jade slowly, holding it in his hands and noting how it was taking on the exact shape of the photographed original, the curves smooth although not yet highly polished, and lacking the decorative etched lines and swirls which would be added as finishing touches.

'It's coming on very well,' he said, replacing it carefully on the bench. 'When will it be finished, do you think?''

'Possibly in a couple of weeks. I'm working on it almost all the time, now.'

He turned slowly to look at her. 'I have another proposition to put to you.'

'Another commission?'

'Not exactly. Let me take you into Hokitika for lunch, and we'll talk about.'

'Thanks for the offer, but I haven't time,' she answered quickly. 'Can't you tell me now?'

'Could we talk about it over a cup of coffee—unless you're unwilling to offer me one?'

Her clear eyes studied him warily. Then she shrugged and let him come with her to the kitchen. Jane was at school because this time he had come on a Tuesday.

Richard watched her, noticed that she was not as deft as usual, and hoped that it was his watching that made her clumsy.

When they were sitting opposite each other, in a pseudo-intimacy that now seemed familiar to him, he saw that perhaps he should have restrained that impulse to nettle her, because the flickering glance she accorded him before lowering her eyes to her cup was hostile.

He pushed his cup away untouched and said, 'Look, I'm not about to leap on you, Alex. Will you stop looking at me like that, and relax?'

'I'm perfectly relaxed. What did you want to talk to me about?'

He restrained his exasperation, only allowing a telling little silence to elapse before he said evenly, 'We—the firm—are engaging in a new venture. We hope to interest some local jewellery craftspeople in designing and making exclusive designs for us. It's to be a special line. You'd have your name on each piece, along with our label. We'd be paying a sort of retainer plus commission on sales. You'd have to give up some of your other work, of course, in order to supply us. We've done some market study, and lined up contacts both here and overseas. We'll also be advertising the new line as something special for the discerning public.'

'You mean it'll be sold on its snob value?'

'Liking and being able to afford beautiful things isn't snobbery. You've got a real chip on your shoulder, haven't you?'

'Perhaps I have. You asked for coffee,' she added, looking pointedly at his cup.

Richard drew it towards him. 'Well? Are you interested?' He was pretending to be occupied in stirring the coffee, but his whole being was tense as he waited for her to answer.

'I don't know,' she said slowly. 'I don't fancy the idea of working for someone else. I value my independence.'

'I'm aware of that. It won't interfere with your independence. In fact, the retainer would increase it, surely? A steady income must be an advantage, particularly with a child to think of.'

Alex looked up at him. 'You're clever, aren't you? You know exactly how to go for the weak spot.'

Holding her eyes, he said, 'I wish I did.'

She wrenched her gaze away, her mouth firming stubbornly.

Richard put out his hand to take her wrist and make her look at him again. He felt her convulsive movement to free herself, and tightened his hold. 'Listen,' he said, 'it's a good deal. Believe me, we genuinely want to promote New Zealand jewellery and craftspeople. Of course we hope and expect to make money out of it. But our terms are fair, I promise you, and it could help your career. It is a career for you, isn't it?'

'Career?' He had caught her interest, and she let her hand lie in his as his grip eased and shifted, apparently forgetting to resist. 'I suppose so. It's a living, of course, but it's more than that. Something I have to do, more like a kind of craving. It's—my life's blood.'

He was staring at her, and she laughed, flushing, and said, 'You don't understand, do you? I didn't expect you to.'

He said, 'You're wrong. No, not wrong. Of course I don't understand completely, because I don't feel like that about my work. But I envy you—and respect your feelings.'

She moved her hand decisively out of his. 'No, you don't,' she said abruptly.

'What does that mean?'

'You don't respect my feelings. Not when they don't fit in with what you happen to want.'

'I see,' he said slowly. 'We're talking about something else, now.'

'No. We're talking about the same thing—in a slightly different context.'

'In that context, then, tell me about your feelings,' he challenged.

'I already have. You didn't want to know.'

'So tell me again. I do want to know. I want to know everything about you.'

'But that's just it!' she sighed. 'You want too damn much, and I can't give it to you.'

'Can't?'

'All right, then—won't. I won't.'

She got up and took the cups, rattling them together and carrying them to the sink. 'I'll think about your business proposition,' she said coldly, with a slight emphasis on 'business.'

She was rinsing the cups, her back to him. Richard pushed his chair away, and his frustration suddenly erupted into anger. In two steps he reached her and caught her arm, meaning only to make her face him, not even aware of how strong his grip was, how violently he was wrenching her round.

Instinctively she hit out at him, her wet hand glancing off his jaw, and he grabbed her wrist, forcing her against the edge of the sink counter. He saw her wide, startled eyes and indignantly parted mouth, and his body came in contact with hers, creating a swift, angry desire. Her head jerked back under his kiss, but he followed through blindly, holding her mouth relentlessly with his, conscious of nothing but the need to make her acknowledge him, to show her that he wouldn't accept her evasions, her refusal to meet his interest in her honestly.

When she moaned under the onslaught of his mouth, his first reaction was pure, primitive pleasure. Then he realised that he must be hurting her, trapped as she was against the counter, his fingers digging into her arm and wrist, and her throat painfully taut.

He released her so suddenly that she clutched at the counter behind her to keep her balance, her breath shuddering from parted lips as she looked at him in furious disbelief.

The hot excitement he still felt mingled with a kind of horror, because he knew that what he had just done was totally wrong, that he had probably wrecked whatever rapport he might have begun to establish between them. His own breathing was harsh, and he tried to calm it before he spoke.

Alex didn't give him a chance. She pushed past him, muttering, 'Get *out* of here!' and left the room so fast he had no time to stop her.

He went after her, and found her in the passageway on the way to her room. She turned as he called her, and said, 'I don't want to talk to you! I told you—get out!'

Richard walked towards her, instead, and her head lifted warily.

'What are you so scared of?' he asked.

With withering scorn, she asked, 'You mean you don't *know*?'

'I'm not a monster, Alex! You don't really think I'd rape you.'

'How would I know?'

'Stop it! You know, all right. I'm not going to touch you.' He stopped in front of her, and said, 'I had no right to do that. I'm sorry.'

'Well, that's nice, I suppose,' she said sarcastically. 'Okay, you've made your apology, your conscience is clear. Now will you just *go*?'

'Let me——'

'No! Leave me alone!'

'Alex, I want to talk——'

'And I don't! I'm telling you again, *no*! I don't want to talk, I don't want to listen to you, I don't want you here, I don't want to *see* you again! Now will you—just—*go—away*?'

Her voice had risen, and, exasperated, he shouted back at her, '*No!*'

She blinked, then her eyes turned glass-hard and emerald with rage. 'This is my house, and I'm telling you to leave. I'm not standing here talking to you any longer.'

She turned and marched to her bedroom, only stopping as she reached the door, because Richard said flatly, 'You go in there, and I'll be right behind you!'

She swung round to face him, blazing, and knew that he meant it.

The telephone was in the hallway, and her eyes found it, before she made a dash for it.

His arm swung up and his hand flattened against the wall to stop her. She came up against him and recoiled, and found herself trapped again, his hands on the wall on either side of her. She looked up and saw the angry pleading in his face, and he said, 'Alex, please!'

'You have no *right*!' she whispered hoarsely, her voice shaking.

Richard closed his eyes, muttering, 'I know, I know. I will go—I promise. But not like this. I can't leave you—hating me.'

He opened his eyes and looked at her, and she saw what was in them. Shaking her head faintly, she said in a barely audible voice, 'I don't hate you, Richard.'

'Alex——' He couldn't quite believe the shimmer in her eyes until he saw the tear slide from one corner. She turned her head, trying to hide it from him, and he leaned over and put his mouth to her skin, licking the salt moisture away with his tongue. 'Alex,' he said softly again, his lips against her cheek. And 'Alex, for God's sake kiss me!' as he found her mouth, found it soft and warm and trembling slightly under his.

His arms went round her, and hers lifted to encircle his shoulders, and the kiss swiftly became a passionate clinging together of lips, arms and thighs, her compliant response sending him a little crazy.

Alex, her head tipped against his arm, her mouth willingly opened to his exploration, felt the sudden thrust of his desire, and her own instinctive, answering movement brought a short, growling sound of pleasure from his throat.

He lifted his mouth and she found herself backed against the wall as he ran his hands over her and watched their passage with absorbed satisfaction. She shuddered under his touch and closed her eyes, savouring the exquisite sensations he was arousing. With her breasts filling his palms, he moved closer again, his mouth slipping over her cheek to her temple and back again, touching her lips with a brief, fierce kiss, then sliding down her throat as she arched it for him, her head thrown back, her eyes still tightly shut. When his tongue settled in the hollow at the base of her throat, she emitted a short, harsh sigh, and he shivered and pulled her close to him. His voice muffled against her skin, he said, 'Darling— where? Your bedroom?'

Alex felt his hold loosen a little as he waited for her to move, to answer. And she went still. Then, with a suddenness that left him stunned, she extricated herself from his embrace, saying, 'No! I—No, I can't!' She ran a hand over her heated cheeks and into her dishevelled hair, and stumbled away from him into the sitting room.

He had followed her in seconds, finding her standing in the middle of the room with her back to him, her arms folded about herself, shoulders rising and falling as she took several deep, steadying breaths. Her head was bent so that her hair hid her face.

Furious and baffled, Richard said roughly, 'No? What the hell are you playing at, Alex? You can't tell me you didn't know what that was leading to?'

Alex flinched and turned to face him, but her eyes didn't meet his. 'Of course I know,' she said huskily. 'But I wasn't thinking straight. I wasn't thinking at all. I'm sorry. My turn to apologise.'

'Sorry! My God, Alex, do you realise what you've done to me?'

Before she could stop herself she shouted at him, 'Yes! You're not the only one, you know!'

She flushed deeply as he stared at her, and looked away from his accusing, comprehending eyes, muttering, 'Look, it was a mistake—I didn't mean it, okay?'

'No, it's not okay! What do you think I am? You can't just pick me up and put me down when you feel like it, my lady! What is it with you? You get your kicks out of that sort of thing? Punishing all of us because of what Jane's father did to you, is that it?'

'Oh, shut up! You're way off beam, anyway. I've told you I'm sorry for denting your masculine pride. You'll get over it.'

'You *bitch*!' he snapped, stung by her contempt.

Alex's eyes widened momentarily, then her face went tight and blank.

'All right,' he conceded angrily, 'I shouldn't have said that.'

She didn't answer, merely shrugging and turning half away from him. Her mouth was set in a stubborn line to stop it trembling.

'You just admitted that you wanted it, too,' he said more calmly. 'Then why won't you let it happen?' She didn't answer, and he said, 'What is it? Moral scruples?'

'Do you think I have any?' she asked bitterly. 'With Jane as evidence against me?'

Feeling his way, he said carefully, 'I've never thought you hadn't any. Is that what's wrong? You still think that I look on you as an easy lay, because you have an illegitimate child?'

'Extramarital,' she said, almost absently.

'What?'

'There's no such thing as legal illegitimacy any more.' Her voice became angry and bitter again. 'At least they've removed *that* label from children like Jane. How can a *child* be illegitimate? So her parents had an "illegitimate" relationship. How could that justify calling her a name like that?'

'There are worse ones.'

'Do you think I don't know that? That *she* doent't?'

'Surely no one would——'

Alex laughed harshly. 'Wouldn't they? What a sheltered life you must have led!'

Irritated, Richard said, 'Shall we get back to the subject under discussion?'

'This is the subject under discussion. Extramarital relationships. That is what you're asking of me, isn't it?'

He hadn't thought of it like that—only that he wanted her fiercely and that for a little while she had seemed to feel the same about him. Had she expected a declaration of his intentions? He wasn't even sure what they were, himself. 'I wanted to make love to you,' he said. 'Are you telling me you wanted some sort of commitment from me, first?' He wasn't sure if he was ready for that. She had kept him deliberately at arm's length for so long. If she had not broken away from him he might have breached the barriers she had set up, but now she was rapidly retreating again behind them.

'I'm telling you that other people can do as they like,' she said, 'but I'm staying strictly celibate. I've been there, thanks, and it's not for me any more. And, what's more important, I don't want to give my daughter a bad example. I would hate her to face what I had to face when I was only really a few years older than she is already. I don't believe any more in sex without marriage. Laugh if you want to.'

'I'm not laughing. I must admit you surprise me. I thought that——'

She looked at him challengingly. 'Yes?'

'You like to be unconventional, you flaunt your life style like a banner. When we first met, you enjoyed trying to shock me. And you could have bought yourself a wedding ring and pretended to be widowed or divorced, for Jane's sake. You've never done that. I thought you were bringing her up to be as liberated as yourself.'

Her look was wryly cynical. 'Liberated! Men have such a peculiar view of that concept. They can't believe it has nothing to do with sex. Oh, I shouldn't blame you, I suppose. Once I thought the pill equated with liberation. But I was young and silly.'

'I didn't say that.'

'It's at the back of your thinking, though. It was behind a lot of the "liberal" ideas that I took note of when I was a teenager. They told us to be "responsible". That meant that if we wanted to have sex, we were to make sure there were no inconvenient consequences for which adults would have to take responsibility. They knew that we were too young to be looking after a baby, but somehow we were not supposed to be too young for a "responsible" relationship with someone just as young, uncertain and mixed up as ourselves. The word was like a chameleon. Every time you looked at it, it had changed its meaning.'

'Were you on the pill?'

'No. In spite of the propaganda, it wasn't so easy to get it then if you were unmarried. I'm not sorry—no matter what they say, it can't be good for young girls, still developing. I wouldn't let Jane . . . We did use something—it was supposed to be reliable.'

'And wasn't.'

'Apparently not. That's when I found out what responsibility really meant.'

'What about the father?'

'He was even more scared than I was. His parents paid for him to take a trip to Australia for a few months until it was all over. He went.'

'The little swine!'

'Oh, no. He was just a boy who couldn't handle it. I'd have run away, too, if I could. It's different for the girl, you see. I want Jane to understand that. You can't run away from it when it happens.'

'You could have had an abortion.'

'If my parents had agreed with abortion, I suppose I might have. I was young enough to go along with what adults decided for me. And I had only the haziest ideas about the life of an unborn child. But I'm profoundly glad that they never suggested it.'

'It must have been rough for you,' Richard commented.

'It was, rather, in spite of my parents' support. Sometimes it still is. I wouldn't want Jane to go through it. I've never lied to her. If I'd tried to keep it secret, she'd have found out eventually, and known that I'd lied. And I was afraid of *how* she might find out—perhaps from someone thoughtless, or downright vindictive. So she knows, and she copes quite well. It isn't such a stigma these days, of course. And we've come through all right, but it hasn't been easy, and— well, for one thing, I never got to university or art school, as I had intended. What I've learned about my craft has been from books or watching other people. A baby changes your life. Even if it's adopted, or aborted, there's no way you can pretend it never existed. I want Jane to know what "responsible" means before she has to learn the hard way.' She stopped and looked at him defiantly, waiting for him to disagree.

'So you haven't allowed a man near you since she was born?'

'I didn't say that. I was only a teenager then. It took a while to really make my mind up. There were one or two men, at different times, that I liked a lot, and—something might have come of it, but a small child tends to hamper an affair. Then there were always the ones who considered me fair game. I suppose that helped to harden my attitude. I just decided that I couldn't recommend one code of conduct to my daughter while I was indulging in quite—well, contrary behaviour.'

Richard looked at her with quiet disbelief. 'For heaven's sake, you're a young woman, you're certainly not abnormal. What did you plan to do for the rest of your life?'

'What spinster ladies used to do before people began thinking sex was indispensable to living. It isn't all that impossible to do without, you know.'

'You mean it hasn't been too hard—until now.'

Her silence acknowledged a hit, and he came closer to her and said, 'You do realise that Jane needn't know?'

She looked at him, and saw that he knew already what her answer would be. His slight smile was wry, and his eyes were shrewd.

Alex shook her head. 'And you realise by now that I won't be dishonest with her. Or anyone.'

'Oh, I don't know about that. You seem to have made an exception in my case.'

Her hand lifted in protest, and dropped. 'What do you mean?'

'You've been evasive from the start, you wouldn't come right out and tell me all this until you were forced into it.'

'How could I? I was hoping there'd be no need——'

'You hoped I'd believe you didn't fancy me, if you kept up the pretence of indifference. It *was* a pretence, wasn't it?'

She bit her lip. 'Yes, I suppose it was, largely. But I was being perfectly honest when I said I didn't want you making love to me.'

His brows went up, and she said, 'It's true! My physical reaction to you has nothing to do with what I really want.'

'Well, at least now you admit there *is* a physical reaction.'

'You know there is. I'm not denying that. And now that your ego has received satisfaction, could we please drop the subject? It's beginning to bore me.'

'Attack is the best mode of defence, isn't it?' Richard said pleasantly, but there was a glint in his eyes which she didn't particularly like. 'You came out fighting the very first time we met,' he went on ruminatively. 'I wonder why?'

'Rubbish! I was very polite, and you were being——'

Alert, and slightly mocking, he said, 'I was being—what?'

'Stuffy,' she said. 'And supercilious.'

He shook his head and said decidedly, 'No. On the defensive, perhaps, because I felt a fool, and you thought I was funny. I suppose I wanted to impress you.'

'No, you didn't. You just wanted to impress on me how superior you were.'

His breath whistled between his teeth. 'You do seem to have gathered some very peculiar first impressions!'

'Didn't *you*?'

'All I remember is that I was annoyed because you were laughing at me. And that wouldn't normally have bothered me. With you, it mattered.'

Sensing dangerous ground, Alex retreated behind another cliché. 'Well, it's all water under the bridge, now, isn't it?' she said.

'And discretion is the better part of valour,' Richard murmured. 'Well, I'll let you get away with it this time.'

Alex gestured vaguely. 'Look, now that you understand, can't we call it quits? I'll let you know when the dragon is finished and send it to you.'

'No. It's too valuable to be trusted to the mails. I'll collect it. And you haven't given me an answer on that other—proposition either.'

'I know. I don't think that in the circumstances it would be a good idea, do you?'

'Are you asking me for my opinion? If so, I think you're being stupid. It has nothing to do with any personal relationship that might or might not develop between us, and you'll only be depriving yourself for no good reason.'

'I simply think we'd be better not seeing each other again.'

'I don't agree. Unless you can't trust yourself to control your emotions when I'm around?'

His grin teased, but there was something in his eyes that wasn't funny.

Acidly, she said, 'I just don't feel like fighting you off all the time. It hasn't escaped me that you're making no promises.'

'You won't have to fight me off, and *that*'s a promise. There are other relationships possible between a man and a woman, you know.'

She looked at him suspiciously, and he said, 'Friendship, for one. Don't you think we could try it?'

'We don't have a lot in common.'

'Alex,' he said, quite gently, 'stop being difficult. I'll come for the dragon when it's ready. You can think about the other in the meantime. Perhaps if I remove my distracting presence you'll be able to come to a sensible decision.'

He put out his hand and caught her chin, giving her face a quick, critical inspection before he bent his head to brush her lips with his. 'Fool!' he muttered softly, and she wasn't sure if he was referring to her or himself. Then he dropped his hand and went out, and Alex was still standing where he had left her, chewing worriedly at her lower lip, when she heard his car leave.

CHAPTER SEVEN

THE school holidays over, Jane was still spending a lot of her free time at the gold claim with Shawn and Paddy, trying to finish projects begun over the Christmas break. It gave Alex time to work without feeling guilty about neglecting her child.

She finished the dragon, deliberately absorbing herself in the work to the exclusion of virtually everything else but Jane. She was almost successful in blotting out the memory of Richard's kisses, but for two days she left the dragon sitting in her workroom before she phoned him to let him know that it was ready.

Richard arrived in his own car while Jane was at school. He smiled easily at Alex, and she found herself smiling back.

'I'm looking forward to seeing it,' he told her as they went together into the workroom.

'I hope you're going to be pleased.'

He glanced at her sharply. 'Any reason why I shouldn't be?'

'No,' she said confidently. 'It's good.'

'I never thought it would be anything else.'

She had covered it with a piece of cloth after the final polishing, and set beside it one of the photographs of the original carving. Now she whipped away the cloth and waited for him to examine the dragon.

He just looked for quite a long time, then carefully picked it up and examined it slowly in his hands, glancing at the photograph and checking it against what she had done with the carving.

'It's perfect,' he said finally, and, in spite of her confidence, her own certainty that she had made a good job of the commission, Alex found herself letting out a relieved breath. 'You're fantastically talented, Alex,' he went on. 'You are going to work for us, aren't you?'

She put out her hands for the carving, and he gave it to her. Turning away a little, she replaced it carefully on the bench. 'It's only a copy,' she shrugged.

'It's terrific, and you know it,' he said forcefully. 'And your own original work is just as beautifully crafted as this. You're an artist with jade. I want to help you, Alex. Let me.'

Her eyes were very green when she finally looked at him. 'As an artist?' she challenged him softly.

'As an artist first and foremost,' he agreed. 'And also as a friend.'

She walked away from him, to lean against the central workbench and look at him consideringly.

'Do you know what?' she said abruptly. 'That vase that I sold you—I could have sold it before, to someone else. I didn't like him.'

'I'm flattered.'

'That's not the point.'

'Then what is?'

'You're going to think this is silly——'

'Try me,' he suggested patiently.

'I don't mind too much, with some things. They're for sale, I sell them. But some things—I put a bit of my soul into them. Like that vase. I wouldn't want you selling them to just anyone who happened to have the right amount of cash. And that's not good business practice, is it? You wouldn't want to lose a customer just because I didn't like him. And anyway, I'd have no control over it, because you're selling my things in Christchurch, or some other city, so how would I know who'd be getting them? You see, I don't generally send special things like that to the shops; I keep them here and sell them—if I sell them—myself. And that's just the sort of thing you want, isn't it? The special pieces?'

'Yes. But there's no law that says I have to sell anything to anyone. It's an agreement made between the buyer and the seller. No agreement, no sale. Would you trust me to vet the buyers?'

She stared at him. 'Yes,' she said slowly. 'Yes, I think I would. But—will you do it?'

'If it's the only way to get you to make things for us, yes. I hope you don't feel that way about too many of the pieces, though. As you say, it wouldn't be good business to refuse a sale too often. As it is, I'll have to work out some tactful formula that will allow us to display things and make them available to the right people.'

'I promise not to do it often.' She stopped, biting her lip, and identified the gleam of triumph in his eyes.

'That's a yes,' said Richard.

'I suppose it is.'

'You might sound more pleased.'

'I'm not sure that I am.'

'You're not selling your soul.'

'Aren't I?'

Slightly exasperated, he said, 'Of course not. What's the matter? Do you feel you're compromising your artistic integrity, or what?'

Alex shrugged unhappily, and he said with some sarcasm, 'I suppose making a decent living with your talent is debasing it! You'd rather be romantically poverty-stricken, would you?'

'It isn't that! And I'm not at all poverty-stricken. We do very well, thanks, without your benevolence!'

He sucked in his breath. 'It's not benevolence, you obstinate, pig-headed woman! It's a business partnership, that's all.'

'Do you usually call your business partners names?'

'No! Only when they——'

He stopped, looking at her suspiciously, his anger dying at the sight of the laughter in her eyes.

Alex giggled, surprising him again. 'Heavens, Richard!' she said. 'It's never going to work. We'd better forget the whole idea.'

'Rubbish! I never let a good idea go to waste. And I won't stand for a talent like yours flowering in the wilderness.'

Her eyes still dancing, she said, 'How poetic of you! But the Coast isn't a wilderness. At least, not all of it. I'm not the only artist working here, you know. It's an inspiration in itself.'

'I know that. You really love it, don't you?'

'I had to come back. It's got a call of its own. Coasters—we just belong here, somehow. I don't think that I could work anywhere else. I learned my trade here, from the old craftsmen, and by steeping myself in the tradition of the coast. The greenstone is here, and I think it loses something if it's taken away to be worked. There used to be a lot of it worked in Germany, you know, before the government stopped it being exported in its raw form. Some of it came back here and was sold as souvenirs, of course. But it's not the same.'

Richard was totally sober now, his eyes almost sombre. 'You're sounding like a mystic,' he said.

Slightly embarrassed, she said, 'Am I? There is something mystical about jade, though. You can't tell me you don't feel it, yourself.'

He laughed a little, acknowledging the truth of that.

Alex smiled back at him serenely. 'I'll wrap the dragon up for you,' she said. 'I hope Mr Mason is going to be pleased, too.'

'I know he will be. Alex, he'd like to meet you.'

'Oh. That's nice of him. Tell him, if he ever comes to the Coast, I'd be delighted.'

'He doesn't travel any more, remember? Will you come back with me to Christchurch? He wants us both to have dinner with him and his wife on Saturday evening. And Marjorie does know you're not a meat-eater, by the way.'

'What?' She stopped wrapping the carving to stare at him.

'He really is keen to meet you. I told him I'd try to persuade you. That's why I brought my car.'

'Why didn't you mention it on the phone?'

'He didn't suggest it until I told him I was coming to fetch the dragon. And I didn't tell you right away because I knew if I asked you on the phone, you'd say no. You would have, wouldn't you?'

'Yes. And it doesn't make any difference, because I'm saying no, anyway. I'd like very much to meet your Mr Mason, but I'm afraid it's impossible. Thank him and tell him——'

'Why is it impossible?'

'Well, because—for all sorts of reasons!'

'Such as?'

'Such as, I'd have to close the studio.'

'We could leave on Saturday after you close the studio. I'll phone tonight and tell them to expect us for dinner.'

'I don't think——'

'And I guarantee to get you on a plane in time to be here Monday morning. You could leave your car at the airport, or get someone to pick you up, if you're too proud to let me pay for a taxi to get you all the way home.'

'I have a child, remember? I can't——'

'Bring her with you. You can both stay with my parents. They like kids.'

'You're very used to getting your own way, aren't you?' Alex sighed.

'Yes. Why does that annoy you?'

'I don't like being ridden over roughshod.'

He frowned. 'I'm not doing that. I'm meeting your rather piffling objections and trying to show you how silly and unnecessary they are. Why don't you be honest and tell me why you really don't want to come?'

'What are you talking about?'

'Oh, come on, Alex,' he said rather wearily. 'The truth is you're plain scared.'

'Scared of what? You? Rubbish!'

'So prove it!'

'Oh, no! That's the oldest trick in the book. I'm not coming, and that's final. Anyway,' she added as a clincher, 'I don't have anything to wear.'

Richard's burst of laughter startled her. She said tartly, 'It happens to be true. I don't own any clothes suitable for dinner with a retired judge.'

'He doesn't expect you to dress up.'

'Look, I'm trying to tell you I have nothing in my wardrobe but shirts, jeans and a couple of faded old skirts.'

'And I'm trying to tell you that it doesn't matter! He's asked to meet you, not your clothes.'

'And how would you feel, taking me along to meet him, you in your five-hundred-dollar suit, and me in my tatty old skirt and a tie-dyed shirt?'

'Proud!' His mouth was set and his eyes dared her to argue.

Her mouth opened to do so, then she faltered and almost smiled. Her voice soft, she said, 'Oh, Richard, that's a very gallant lie! Thank you.'

'It was not a lie!' he snapped furiously. 'I don't give a damn what you wear, and neither will Justice Mason. Your trouble is you're a sham and a fraud. Underneath that trendy, artistic pose of yours, you've a conventional streak a mile wide! "I haven't a thing to wear!"' he mimicked cruelly. 'The only one who cares is you!'

'Don't you dare accuse me of posing!' she snapped.

'Does that hurt?' He sounded jeering, but his face abruptly changed as he said, 'Oh, God, Alex, I don't want to fight with you. Stop making excuses and say you'll come.'

His volte-face shook her. Suddenly unbearably tempted, she wailed, 'No-o! I won't let you——'

'Let me what?'

'Manipulate me! You're too good at it.'

'I swear,' he said, 'I'm not trying to manipulate you. I'm asking you, Alex. Just asking. Will you come with me, to make an old man happy? I promise you there are absolutely no hidden strings attached.'

He looked perfectly serious, and she found his quiet tones very persuasive.

Still not really sure that he wasn't being terribly clever, she sighed, shrugged and finally agreed.

Jane didn't come with her, after all. Paddy was engaged in building a replica of a nineteenth-century miner's hut, with the help of Jane and Shawn, and not even the prospect of a long trip in Richard's car could compete with the attraction of hammers and nails and the satisfaction of seeing a real building grow under their hands. 'Besides,' she told her mother, 'we want to finish it before Easter, and we've still got all the inside to do, and the furniture to fix. Paddy and Shawn can't do it on their own.'

'We'd only be away a couple of days,' Alex reminded her.

'Yes, but we can do a lot in that time. We're almost ready for the roof, now, and they'll need me for that.'

Alex forbore to smile. Jane might be only nine, but she was a very capable little person, and although Paddy could no doubt have done the whole thing himself, she had little doubt that the children really were helping.

Seeing her wavering, Jane said, 'I can stay with the Terawitis—they won't mind.'

'How do you know?' Alex asked, without conviction. She knew very well that Charlotte would have Jane any time, and that Jane would be perfectly safe and happy there.

Jane grinned. 'They love me!' she said cockily.

'I can't imagine why!' Alex lifted her eyes.

Jane made a face at her and retreated, squealing with laughter as Alex aimed a slap at her denim-covered little bottom.

The whole country was in the grip of a drought, but Westland had felt it less than most places. Although there were areas of dry grass on the hills, the forest still remained green, and the swampy lowlands retained an appearance of lushness. Richard drove carefully over the tortuous bends and twists of Arthur's Pass, and across a broad shingly river bed with the blue water a narrow ribbon threading its way between misty hills like a Victorian landscape painting. A soft drizzle fell, adding to the ethereal quality of the scene. But once they had descended out of the damp forest on the other side of the mountains, into the less exciting but much safer terrain of rolling grass-covered hills and outcropping grey rock, the effects of the lack of rain here were startling. Not a hint of green showed anywhere, the dry browns and straw-golds of the countryside more typical of the Australian outback than of New Zealand's 'grand hills for sheep'.

In Christchurch itself the heat was scorching, the city lying grey and parched in the grip of an iron sun. Even the grass along the banks of the Avon that wound its lazy way through the city looked tired and flat.

'I didn't realise,' said Alex, 'how bad the drought is. The farmers must be going crazy.'

'They are,' Richard told her. 'Not that I know many farmers, but I've seen them on TV, and it doesn't take too much imagination to guess what's happening to the land and think what it must mean to them. It's a tough year.'

'And February isn't over yet,' Alex murmured, appalled.

'We'd all be glad to see some rain. One thing about a drought, it makes you appreciate what we normally think of as a spot of bad weather.'

'You're city bred,' Alex accused teasingly. 'Us country folk never turn up our noses at a bit of rain.'

He slanted a gleaming look at her. 'Really?'

He sounded so sceptical that she stared at him, puzzled. 'Why do you say it like that?'

He shrugged. 'I was just making a sort of analogy. You wouldn't appreciate it.'

It took her a minute to connect. Then her cheeks burned. 'I'm not a drought victim,' she said. Without thinking, she added, 'Anyway, you're hardly a spot of rain. More like a raging thunderstorm!'

'Well, well!' he said softly, as she sat furiously wishing she had simply held her tongue and pretended not to have any idea what analogy he had been thinking of. His mouth curved in a self-satisfied smile. 'Thank you, Alex. You've given me hope.'

'Don't count on it!' she snapped.

He laughed. 'I wouldn't count on anything with you. You enjoy keeping me off balance, don't you?'

'I've no idea what you're talking about.'

He negotiated a traffic intersection, turning away from the riverbank they had been following, towards the centre of the city where the cathedral spire pinned the sky ahead of them. 'Yes, you have,' he said calmly. He swung the car left, picking up speed. 'You may not want to have a love affair, but you find the possibility intriguing all the same. You don't really want to be "just friends" any more than I do. You're constantly challenging me, sending out signals and then retreating as soon as I look like taking you up on them.'

About to deny it hotly, Alex hesitated, trying to be honest with herself. That remark about him being like a thunderstorm had undoubtedly been provocative, although unpremeditated. Sometimes when their glances collided, she had found it difficult to wrench hers away from the silent message in his. She knew that the sexual tension between them was as strong as ever. They had spent the afternoon together in the confined space of the car, and she was aware of his every movement, every subtle tone of his voice when he spoke. She had sensed that he, too, was equally aware of her. In spite of herself, she had enjoyed knowing that when her thigh accidentally brushed his as she turned to get her bag from the back seat, his jaw muscles had clamped tight, that when they had stopped at a wayside café for a drink, and she stepped back suddenly against him as someone came hurriedly through the narrow doorway, a tremor had run through his body while he held her momentarily with his hand on her wrist.

Had she been sending out signals, even semi-subconscious ones? 'I don't mean to,' she said. 'If I have, I'm sorry.'

Richard didn't respond, and after a few minutes he slowed and entered a driveway between a pair of old-fashioned concrete pillars. The house was quite small, although it had two storeys, and the garden that surrounded it was well-established and obviously meticulously cared for, with a semi-circle of green lawn enclosed by the drive, and a medley of flowering shrubs giving privacy from the neighbours.

'You live here?' she asked him as he drew up behind a small, new Japanese car parked in the carport adjacent to the house.

'More or less,' he said. 'I have a place of my own at Akaroa where I often spend weekends, but during the week I generally stay here with my parents.'

'They are expecting me, aren't they?' Alex asked, suddenly nervous.

'I said that I might bring a visitor, possibly two for the night, and that we'd be out for dinner. Like the Masons, they're half expecting you.'

He leaned over to open her door, and she asked, 'What have you told them about me?'

He unlatched the door and sat back just a little, so that he was still close to her. 'That you're a talented lady, and that I'd like them to meet you.'

'Is that all?'

'Yes.'

She looked away, and he said, 'What's the matter?'

'Nothing.' She made a move to get out of the car, but he stopped her with a hand on her shoulder.

'What have I said?' he demanded, frowning.

'You haven't said a thing!'

She made an attempt to avoid his hand, but his fingers only tightened, holding her.

Slowly he asked, 'Then what was I supposed to have said? That you're an unmarried mother? Is that it?'

'Well, why didn't you?' she asked him.

'Because it's *irrelevant*, that's why!'

She looked at him searchingly, and he said, 'Did you expect me to have given them your life story?'

'No, of course not. I just wondered——'

'You wondered what sort of reception you'd get if they knew?'   ·

'In a way. I don't want to accept hospitality under false pretences.'

'What do you want to do? March in and say to my mother, 'Hello, I'm Alex—I have a nine-year-old daughter and I'm not married''?'

She couldn't help smiling ruefully as she shook her head. 'Of course not. But if I did, would it shock her?'

She could see he was about to say no, but she held his eyes with hers, and he paused, then said soberly, 'I suppose it might, a bit. She has traditional ideals about sex and marriage, but she's a very intelligent woman, far too much so to judge people hastily, or to fail to make allowances for changed social standards. And certainly she wouldn't show you the door because of it. I should have added that she has a lot of compassion and understanding.'

Glad that he had answered her truthfully, she said, 'I won't deliberately set out to shock her. But I refuse to treat Jane as a shameful secret.'

'No one expects you to. You're too sensitive on the subject.'

'Am I? Maybe you're right.'

He smiled down at her, and said, 'I like it when you sound humble. It makes a change.'

He bent closer, his eyes on her lips, and she jerked her head aside. Instantly the tension that had almost disappeared returned with a snap. She felt his breath on her cheek, and the strength of his fingers on her shoulder. She knew that he was fighting the desire to use force, to make her turn and accept his kiss, and that if he did, it wouldn't be the light, gentle caress he had first intended, but something quite different.

Then his hand slid from her shoulder and he moved back. In a chilly, remote voice, he said, 'Come on out, then. I'll bring your bag.'

His mother was certainly not formidable. She had a fadedly pretty face and lively blue eyes alight with the intelligence her son had mentioned. Her greeting was friendly and warm without being over-effusive, and Alex liked her at once. Richard's father, not as tall as his son, and much more gentle in manner, regarded her shrewdly and cast Richard a speculative glance as he shook her hand firmly and welcomed her. He held her fingers in his for a few more seconds, and nodded before releasing them. 'Good hands,' he said. 'I'm not surprised that your jade work is excellent.'

Alex smiled, and Richard explained, 'My father believes he can recognise the hands of a craftsman. He used to choose his apprentices on the basis of that instinct.'

'Not instinct,' Mr Lewis corrected him. 'Knowledge.'

'Do you make jewellery, Mr Lewis?' Alex asked.

'I used to, but my eyes aren't what they were.'

'And Richard? Didn't he ever try it?'

'I lack the hands,' Richard said solemnly.

His father snorted. 'He lacked the inclination as well as the hands. Not enough patience.'

'And not enough talent. I prefer business

administration,' said Richard. 'It provides me
with all the challenge I need.'

Alex sent him a swift, sparkling glance, then
quickly looked away.

Mrs Lewis said, 'Show Alex to Rosemary's
room, Richard. She'll want to change and freshen
up, I suppose. Then perhaps you'd both like a
small sherry before you go off for dinner.'

Richard said, 'I don't know if Alex drinks——'

'That would be lovely, thank you,' Alex
interrupted firmly. And as he picked up her case
and preceded her down the wide hall, she said to
him,' What made you think I was a teetotaller?'

'I said I didn't know if you were or not,' he
reminded her, stopping at the door of one of the
rooms. 'Here.' He pushed it open and walked in,
depositing her case on the pretty floral bedspread.
'This used to be my sister's room, until she got
married to a North Islander and went to live in
Auckland.'

As she looked about appreciatively at the pale
primrose wallpaper and rosewood furniture, he
added, 'I thought that maybe your vegetarianism
went with eschewing the demon drink as well.'

'I don't drink a lot, but I like a good wine.'

'Mr Mason will be pleased. He prides himself
on being something of a connoisseur.'

'Oh, I'm not that! But I hope I'll be able to do
justice to his taste.'

'You'd do justice to any man's taste.'

The compliment took her unawares. After a
moment, she said, 'Thank you.' She walked to
the window and touched the curtains that
matched the bedspread. 'This is a very nice
room. You've a lovely home.'

'Are you blushing?' he asked, amused.

'No, of course not.' But she didn't face him, and he said, 'The bathroom's just across the hall. My room is next door, by the way, and my parents sleep upstairs.'

'Oh.' She turned then, a little surprised, a little wary.

'Don't worry,' he said quite gently. 'I won't make any advances if you don't.'

Her eyes flashed at that, and he laughed. 'Well, if you've got everything you need——' he said, moving towards the door.

'Everything, thank you,' she said with firm emphasis, and he grinned and went out, shutting the door behind him.

Alex had been telling him the truth about her wardrobe, but she had made an effort for tonight, resurrecting a garment she had not worn for years, a caftan in fine cream Indian muslin with heavy embroidery round the plunging neckline and full sleeves. It wasn't the height of fashion, but it was a style that hardly dated, and she had washed and ironed it carefully, and in a flash of inspiration sewn a series of tiny jade tear-shaped cabuchons on to the embroidery at the neckline, so that they swung slightly each time she moved. She clasped about her neck a gold chain holding an intricate jade carving of her own design, and smoothed on some green eye-shadow she had hunted out from the bottom of one of her dressing-table drawers that morning, and a smidgeon of lipstick rescued from a box in Jane's room that held 'dress-up' clothes among other odds and ends. There was nothing she could do with her hair except brush it until it crackled, and let it fall in a shining, soft curtain about her face.

When she entered the lounge, Richard was

already there with his parents, and she saw the slight shock in his eyes as he stood up and came towards her to lead her to a chair. He ran his eyes swiftly over her, and she smiled at his surprise, unable to hide her pleasure in it.

He seated her on the sofa opposite his parents, and said to them, 'This is the girl who told me she didn't have a thing to wear!'

'You look lovely, dear,' his mother said, as he went to a cupboard in one corner and asked, 'Sweet, medium or dry? Or would you rather have a cocktail?'

'Medium, please,' she answered.

He poured it and brought it over to her. As she leaned forward to take it, she looked enquiringly at him, because he stood with the glass in his fingers without making any move to give it to her. He was looking at the neckline of her gown, his eyes glittering, and she leaned back suddenly against the sofa, startled and embarrassed.

He moved then, his eyes going to her face as he held out the glass, and she took it carefully, afraid of spilling the sherry on the cream muslin because her hand was shaking.

She sipped at the liquid, grateful to have an excuse to cast her eyes down, while Richard sat beside her and said evenly, 'That's a lovely piece of jade you're wearing. Made it yourself, I suppose?'

'Yes. Yes, I did.' Her left hand went up to touch it, and to hide the bared skin and the shadowed cleft that he had seen as he stood over her.

'May I see?' he asked very politely.

She raised her eyes, and saw that his were

laughing, the disquieting glitter under control now.

'Of course,' she said, equally polite, because she could hardly refuse in front of his parents. She lifted the chain, about to slip it off, but he said smoothly, 'Don't spoil your hair,' and slid across the sofa to her, his fingers taking the slight weight of the ornament, his russet head close as he studied it.

'Very nice,' he murmured, then, lifting his eyes to hers, unmistakably teasing, he said, 'Beautifully made.'

He replaced it, tucking it into the neckline of the caftan, his knuckles brushing her skin intimately, and Alex gritted her teeth and said, 'Thank you,' as coolly as her suddenly husky voice would allow.

His father said, 'Richard was quite excited about your work when he first went to the West Coast. I'm very glad you've decided to do some pieces for us.'

With relief she turned to the older man, but Richard hadn't moved back to the other end of the sofa, and she was very conscious of his thigh lightly touching hers, his arm against her shoulder. Determinedly she ignored him while she chatted to his parents, and then as she finished her drink, he glanced at his watch and said, 'Time for us to go, I'm afraid. Do you need some sort of wrap or anything, Alex?'

She shook her head and reluctantly rose.

'Don't wait up for us, will you?' Richard said to his parents, and his mother laughed and replied, 'We gave that up years ago, and you know it. Have a good time, both of you.'

In the car the atmosphere was electric. Trying to lighten it, Alex asked, 'Do we have far to go?'

'It'll take about fifteen minutes. Do you like my parents?'

'Very much. I think they're nice people. You're lucky.'

'Do you miss yours?'

'Not often now. I'm glad I've got Jane, though.'

'Everybody needs somebody?'

'Yes, I suppose so.'

'Supposing I told you I need you?' he said.

'I'd say I've heard that line before.'

He was angry, and she knew it. But he laughed softly and said, 'You've heard them all before, haven't you? Don't you believe in sincerity any more?'

'I don't believe that you need anyone. You're a very self-confident man. I don't see you in *need* of any woman.'

'You'd be right, there.' He sounded almost savage, and she blinked. 'You don't need anyone, either, do you?' he said. 'You're very self-sufficient, *Ms* Cameron. All independence and liberated womanhood.'

Alex laughed. 'It really bugs you, doesn't it? You hate the thought of a woman being able to get along without a man! My God, scratch a middle-class liberal, and you're sure to find a male chauvinist pig lurking under the skin!'

He had to stop for a red light, and as he twisted in his seat to face her, she caught her breath at the cold rage that glittered at her. 'You're really asking for it, aren't you, Alex?' he said in a voice that was dangerously pleasant. 'And before very long, it will be my very great pleasure to make sure that you get it!'

The red signal changed to green, and he

returned his attention to the car, driving smoothly and in silence until he pulled up outside a house with a broad lawn sweeping down to the footpath, and a welcoming light shining on the porch.

CHAPTER EIGHT

ALEX would not have believed she could have enjoyed herself so much after that exchange with Richard in the car. But she found Justice Mason a delightful and witty old man, and his wife, Marjorie, was warm and interesting. In her late forties, she was still a very beautiful woman, but it took only a short time for Alex to realise that it was certainly not just for her looks that Mr Mason had married her.

When Richard handed him the box containing the dragon, she watched eagerly for his reactions. He pushed aside the tissue paper and lifted the carving out, held it in his hand with his white head bent, then said, his voice shaking a little, 'Marjorie.'

His wife, who had been sitting beside Alex on the sofa, immediately got up and went to perch on the arm of the Judge's chair, her hand on his shoulder.

'I've got my dragon back!' He held it up to show her, and Alex caught the glimmer of tears in his eyes, and the loving understanding in the smile Marjorie gave him as she took the jade. For a few moments they admired it, then the old man looked across at Alex and said, 'Thank you. I don't think I would have known it from the original. I suppose it's silly of me to care so much for an inanimate object, but it broke my heart when the dragon was stolen from me. You've done a wonderful job.'

'I'm glad you're pleased,' she answered. And Richard, sitting across from her, raised the glass his host had given him in a silent toast, smiling at her.

'You should thank Richard,' she said. 'He persuaded me to do it.'

'I do.' Mr Mason nodded courteously in his direction. 'And now I'm going to put this little fellow where he belongs.'

He rose and went to a carved Oriental table in one corner of the large, beautifully-furnished lounge, to place the dragon carefully on the inlaid surface.

Turning to Alex, he said, 'I hope you approve?'

'Very much.' She got up, too, and went to study the effect at close quarters. 'Is this where the other one was kept?'

'Yes. I daresay I should have locked it away, but I've always believed that lovely things should be seen and appreciated.'

'Alex would agree with you,' said Richard, coming to join them. 'She even chided me for putting her vase that I showed you in my bedroom, keeping it to myself.'

'I didn't chide you!' she protested.

'Well—questioned my choice,' he amended, smiling provocatively at her.

Alex shook her head, refusing to argue, and returned to the sofa as Marjorie excused herself to check on the dinner. Richard followed her, murmuring, 'Don't be annoyed—I wasn't getting at you.'

'I'm not.' She sat down, and found him ensconcing himself beside her.

'Sure?' he asked her softly.

'Quite sure.'

'Then could you bring yourself to smile at me, do you think?'

She looked up, and found him looking back at her so quizzically that she smiled without even thinking about it.

'Beautiful!' he said with satisfaction, making her laugh. He grinned back over his drink and said, 'Enjoy yourself.'

She did. The meal Marjorie had made was superb, and the wine that went with it was equally so. When Alex diffidently hoped that her preferences had not posed problems for her hostess, Marjorie laughed and said, 'Good heavens, no! I enjoy vegetarian food, too, and collect special recipes to serve my vegetarian friends, though I have to admit that I'm too partial to the taste of meat, myself, to join them on a permanent basis.'

The conversation after dinner sparkled with wit and good feeling, and it was long after midnight when their hosts allowed them to take their reluctant leave.

Richard drove straight home through the quiet streets, whistling softly to himself, as Alex sat beside him enjoying a pleasant, slightly sleepy euphoria.

'Glad you came after all?' he asked her when they stopped outside his home.

A smile hovered on her mouth. 'You Shylock!' she said.

'How am I a Shylock?'

'Want your pound of flesh, don't you? All right, I admit I'm glad I met Mr Mason, and his wife is super, and I had a thoroughly good time. Satisfied?'

'It's a handsome admission. I enjoyed the evening too. Shall we bring it to its natural conclusion?'

'Richard——'

'Alex——' he mimicked her. 'One kiss, here in the car, is all I'm suggesting. No big seduction scene, I promise.'

'I don't think——'

'I do,' he said, and reached for her, not roughly, and not so firmly that she couldn't have stopped him.

She didn't. She wanted his arms about her, liked the feel of him against her, the way his fingers slid from her shoulder to her nape and into her hair, cradling her head for a moment against his upper arm while his lips grazed her temple.

'I've had too much wine,' she said feebly, and felt his breath of laughter against her skin.

'No, you haven't. Why do you need excuses?'

He gave her no chance to answer, but tipped her chin with his hand and kissed her, his mouth surprisingly soft against her lips. He took her upper lip between his, first, gently nibbling, and then opened his mouth over hers with slow, leisurely movements, coaxing her lips apart until her breath sighed into his throat. His other hand was stroking her neck, his fingertip tracing the line of her throat down into the opening of the caftan, until the greenstone pendant stopped him.

She felt him lift it, his mouth still moving on hers, then his hand slipped beneath the pendant and his fingers splayed over her breast.

Her heart jolted, and for an instant of hot, confused yearning she left his hand there before she lifted hers and clamped it on his wrist, at the same time trying to reject his mouth.

'All right, it's all right,' he murmured against her lips, and his hand shifted to her throat, her chin, holding her. He began caressing her throat again, and her cheek, as his mouth insisted on retaining its possession of hers, with an insidious, persuasive pressure.

When she felt a shudder pass through him, and his arms tightened about her, she realised that they were rapidly reaching the point of no return, and with an effort began to push away from him.

For a few seconds he took no notice, but then he let her go abruptly, and gripped the steering wheel, his breathing harsh.

Alex sat with clenched hands, trying to steady her own breathing.

Richard let out a deep, unsteady sigh, relaxed back against the seat, and sent her a gleaming glance. 'Thank you,' he said. 'I didn't think you'd give me so much.'

'I didn't mean to,' she confessed huskily. 'You certainly took advantage of a goodnight kiss!'

'I wasn't the only one, though, was I?' he enquired, with deadly teasing.

Alex closed her eyes, then made a helpless little gesture of capitulation. 'No,' she admitted.

He laughed quietly and put up a hand, turning her face to his. 'I love you,' he said softly, and kissed her briefly on the lips.

He released her immediately and got out of the car, opening her door while she was still trying to digest that, wondering how much he meant by it.

He steered her inside with his hand touching her waist, and at her bedroom door he leaned in to switch on the light. 'Stop looking so nervous,' he admonished her, noting her wide eyes and the mask she was trying to fix on her face. 'I'm not even going to try. I promised, didn't I?'

'Goodnight, then,' she said woodenly, and he smiled at her.

'Goodnight, darling.'

Alex woke quite early, although the bed was comfortable and she had slept soundly.

She felt good, wide awake almost at once, and was conscious of a curious sense of happy anticipation, like the night before Christmas when she was a child.

Not stopping to analyse the feeling, she threw back the covers and put on the faded cotton wrapper which was the only cover-up garment she owned. Picking up her toilet things in their plastic lunch bag, she made for the bathroom.

The shower was warm and refreshing, and after it she pulled the wrapper on over her bare skin before opening the door.

Richard was leaning in the doorway of his own room, dressed already and waiting for her. 'Come here,' he said. 'I want to show you something.'

'Can't it wait a while?' She edged to her own door.

He came over to her, took the bag from her hand, and tossed it on the unmade bed. 'It won't last,' he said firmly, taking her arm. 'Come on.'

Mystified, she went with him to his room. At the doorway she held back a little, but he tightened his grip and made her enter.

Then she saw it.

The room was on a corner of the house, and the bed had been placed against the main window, but on the other outside wall was a high, small window with leadlight panes, and in the embrasure stood her jade vase. The early sun was behind it, lending an ethereal glow to the translucent green stone. The delicate carved edges shimmered, and every flowing line was accentuated by the pearly light. She had carved it herself, but she felt her eyes prick with tears at the beauty of it, and she was filled with a kind of surprised wonder that she had been able to make anything so startlingly lovely.

Richard was standing silently just behind her. His hands came to her waist and he held her lightly, his body just touching hers. His cheek against her hair, he said very softly, 'Gorgeous, isn't it? Thank you, Alex.'

'You paid for it,' she reminded him, trying to ignore a strong desire to lean back against him and place her hands over his to guide them into a more intimate embrace.

As if he had read her thoughts, he shifted, bringing her closer, and one hand slid to her breast, the fingers curving under the gentle swell of it, and the thumb slipping inside the edge of her wrapper to caress her skin.

'Don't,' she whispered.

'You smell of soap and morning,' he murmured against her neck, pushing aside the robe to bare her shoulder to his mouth.

His lips were warm and firm, and started a delighted shiver that she couldn't hide.

She heard him laugh with quiet triumph, then he turned her in his arms and found her mouth in a long, hard, dizzying kiss.

And Alex kissed him back unreservedly, her hands on his shoulders, her head tipped against his arm, her mouth eagerly accepting his.

When he stopped kissing her, she opened her eyes and looked at the triumph in his with bemusement. He smiled, and she bit her lip, looking away, pushing against him as her hands slid to his chest.

He began, 'Alex——'

And then she heard someone coming down the stairs, and reacted with a sudden stiffening of her body, a sharply indrawn breath as she realised how they would look if his mother or father caught a glimpse of them through the open door.

'Let go!' she whispered as he still held her.

His eyes contracted in surprise. He took in the embarrassment on her face, and grinned. 'I said you had a conventional streak, didn't I?'

He retained his hold on her waist, and went to the door, flinging it wide to call, 'Good morning, Mother!'

His mother, just at the foot of the stairs, hesitated. She looked from Richard to Alex, and a flicker of surprise crossed her face.

Richard said easily, 'I've been showing Alex her vase—the one I bought from her.'

Mrs Lewis's features relaxed immediately. 'Oh, yes. With the sun on it, it's very beautiful. He's tremendously fond of it, you know, Alex. Now, what do you like for breakfast? I have fruit juice, toast and coffee, but the men prefer bacon and eggs. Which will you have?'

Alex moved from Richard's encircling arm and said, 'I'll join you in toast and coffee if I may, Mrs Lewis, when I'm dressed.'

'There's no hurry, dear. Whever you're ready.'

Mrs Lewis proceeded on her way to the kitchen, and Alex, without a backward glance at Richard, hurried to her room.

There was no more chance for any private conversation until he took her to the airport for her flight back to the Coast. And then he didn't seem inclined to talk, driving with a frowning abstraction while Alex sat taut and uneasy beside him, trying to think of small talk, and finding her tongue tied by a paralysing sense of unsureness.

In the departure lounge she checked her bag and then they hung about with the other passengers and their friends and families, Alex silent and increasingly unhappy, and Richard equally silent, and forbiddingly grim-looking.

At last he gave a short, exasperated sigh and, taking her arm, steered her into a quiet corner away from other people. 'Listen,' he said urgently, 'I'll come next week. We have to talk.'

She stared at him, opened her lips to speak, then heard her flight called over the loudspeaker.

'Oh, hell!' Richard said softly. His hands closed on her shoulders, his eyes were intense with emotion. 'Tell me you love me, Alex,' he muttered.

Her eyes dilated, her heart plunging in fright. She felt his hands tighten painfully. 'Tell me!' he insisted.

But she wasn't ready for that. Dumbly she shook her head.

'*Alex!*'

'I—can't!' she whispered. 'Richard, let me go. My plane——'

'Damn the plane. And damn you, Alex! You kissed me as though you loved me!'

The boarding call came again, and her eyes went past him. He drew in his breath quickly and bent his head, kissing her fiercely, ignoring her instinctive recoil. His mouth claimed hers without mercy for a few moments, then he stepped back, his face taut with frustrated desire and his eyes glittering. 'Next week,' he said, making it sound like a threat. She felt his eyes following her as she walked to the plane.

But he didn't come the following week. Instead he phoned with the news that his father had suffered a stroke and was in hospital. He sounded clipped and unemotional as he answered her shocked questions. The doctors believed that his father would recover, but he would need to take things easy for some time, very likely for the rest of his life. It wasn't possible for Richard to leave him and his mother at the moment.

'Of course not,' Alex agreed at once, conscious of a curious relief.

Perhaps he sensed it. 'Don't break your heart, will you?' he said dryly. When she didn't answer, he added, 'I'll be in touch. Take care.'

'Yes,' she replied automatically. 'You too. Please give my sympathy to your mother and father.'

She sent a Get Well card to the hospital, and wrote to Mrs Lewis offering what comfort she could. It seemed inadequate, but the best she could do.

After two weeks, Richard phoned again. His father was going to be all right, was expected to be able to walk with a stick, but would need therapy for some time. They thought he would be home from the hospital in a week or two. In the meantime, Richard was snowed under with business, doing his father's work as well as his own. 'Are you all right?' he asked. 'And working?'

'Yes,' she said. 'I've been making some pendants from the jade you bought for the dragon.'

'Your own designs?'

'Yes, some new ones.'

'I'd like to see them.'

'I'll send them to you when I've finished.'

'Bring them,' he suggested.

Alex hesitated. 'I'll send them,' she repeated. 'By registered post.'

'I want to see you, Alex.'

Her hand clenched on the receiver. She couldn't answer him.

Richard sighed sharply. 'All right—send them. I'll come as soon as I can.'

He wrote to her later. The letter detailed his father's progress ('better than anyone expected, but it will be a while before he's able to work at all') and reiterated his promise to come as soon as he could. 'We have things to say, Alex, that can't very well be said on the phone or in a letter.' Above the signature he had scrawled, 'I love you.'

When she read it, she crumpled the letter in her hand, hesitated, then tossed it away in the wastebasket in her studio. A sense of warmth and excitement was succeeded by panic. Alex lashed herself deliberately into anger. The arrogance of men! A few kisses in an unguarded moment and they thought a woman was theirs for the taking. She had never said she loved him. And what did he want for his love? What did he even mean by it?

We have things to say . . .

What did he expect her to say? What he had asked her to say at the airport? *I love you . . .*

She remembered his kiss, and felt a stirring of hot, sweet desire.

But desire was a trap.

And so could love be. She didn't want his love. She didn't want to desire him. A boat-rocker—she had labelled him that the very first time they met. And she had been right. Let him stay away, safely away from her. Let her forget him, be content again as she had been before he came.

But in the night, when she hadn't Jane to distract her, hadn't the jade to busy her hands and absorb her mind, she lay lonely and wakeful and restless.

Wanting him.

CHAPTER NINE

ALEX wanted to carve a heron. The image of the one they had seen stalking the edge of the lake on the way to the glaciers had stayed with her, transforming itself in her mind into a jade figure, graceful, freely-formed and opalescent. Her fingers ached to translate the image into reality, but she had no suitable stone. All the jade she had was too green. The *kotuku*, the legendary, mystical white heron, cried out for a nearly white stone.

Such jade was uncommon. She had once seen a Chinese ornament in Khotan nephrite, milky white with the merest hint of green, and sometimes a boulder of Inanga was found with a hard white crust, but this tended to be opaque or mottled.

She put out feelers, looked about the back rooms of the jade factories, and even strolled along the beaches, hoping for a lucky find among the stones washed from the river mouths into the sea and ashore again. She and Jane spent a couple of days on the banks of the Taramakau and its tributaries, fossicking for the elusive stone without success.

Then Paddy told her he had heard of a carver down at Franz Josef who had a piece of white jade that he was willing to sell.

'I want true jade,' Alex said doubtfully. 'If he found it farther south, it's probably bowenite.'

Paddy shrugged. 'Looks just as good to me.

The Maoris used it. Called it *Tangiwai*, weeping water.'

'Stop showing off your knowledge,' Alex grinned. 'I know that, too. I suppose I could use it, if it's really good quality. The stuff's hard enough, but it doesn't work like nephrite. Some of it's beautifully white and clear, though.'

'Suit yourself,' Paddy shrugged. 'Why don't you go down and see, anyway?'

'Yes, I might,' she said slowly. 'I could do it in a day trip, and I'd hate to miss out if it is what I'm looking for.'

She went the following day, arranging for Jane to go to Shawn's house after school in case she was late for any reason. Drought still held most of the country in its grip. Canterbury sweltered in a heatwave. But on the Coast, it was raining.

Alex found the carver in his workshop, and examined the jade—a smallish slab, cut, he said, from a piece found at Lake Wakatipu. It could be true jade, then. Only a chemical analysis would disclose that for sure, but she would know when she began to work with it. It was the right size, the right colour, and it had the translucent quality she wanted for the *kotuku*. She bought it, and left well satisfied with her purchase.

But it had taken longer than she had expected to find the carver. Instead of being in the township, he had his studio down a side road studded with little bridges and shallow fords, and within sight of the broad slate-blue river flowing from the glacier. His wife kept a small souvenir shop in the town, he explained, and did the selling while he worked in peace in his private retreat. He kept her talking, in spite of his stated preference for a lonely life, and it was well after two when Alex climbed into the VW, thinking that it would be dark by the time she reached home, and that it was just as well she had made arrangements for Jane to stay at the Terawitis until she arrived back.

At the first bridge, she was a little alarmed to see the height of the water in the stream that joined the river further down. It rushed through only inches below the boards, and had obviously risen considerably since she had come this way a couple of hours ago.

By the time she had crossed a ford, her heart in her mouth in case the little car didn't make it through the water that splashed up to the windows as she roared through, she was seriously concerned. And a little farther on she found, with a sickening lurch of despair, a bridge that had been unable to withstand the flood and been washed out, the water slewing its old timbers sideways, and gouging out a hole in the bank that made the road completely impassable.

Dismayed, Alex sat gripping the steering wheel, realising that she wasn't going to get home tonight. The carver's cottage was the only habitation she had seen on the road, and if she didn't make it back across the ford, she was in for a long, cold night in the car.

With some difficulty she turned the car again on the narrow, roughly surfaced road, and grimly drove back.

The ford looked dangerously high, the icy water racing and leaping on its way to the river. She didn't dare try to cross it, imagining the car being borne away by the flood, herself helpless inside.

She returned to the bridge, hoping that the carver's wife or someone else might come along, and at least be able to get a message to Jane and the Terawitis for her. She parked on the highest ground she could find, and rummaged for the extra jersey she had fortunately thrown on the back seat, anticipating a cold wind coming off the glacier, and the rug which was always kept in the back.

Then there was nothing to do but keep as warm as she could, and wait.

No one came. Perhaps the road was impassable farther down, too. When it got dark, she made herself get out of the car for a few minutes, into the chilly, wet air, and tried to ease some of the stiffness from her legs.

When she crawled back in on to the back seat, her feet were cold, but she was wearing jeans which kept her legs covered, her jersey was wool, and the blanket cosy. She felt chilled but not frozen. She tried to sleep.

It wasn't easy. In the night the rain came down in torrents, and there were ominous sounds of trees cracking and tearing, of floodwaters roaring down the valley. Alex wondered how high the rivers would run, if she was still safe from the flood. At the storm's height, the night pitch black outside and the sounds of its fury assaulting her ears continuously in a menacing cacophony, she huddled into the blanket with her heart seeming to climb into her throat, shivering with cold and fear. She supposed she might die here, swept away by the rising waters, or crushed under a falling tree. She brushed away a tear, thinking of Jane left alone without her. And she thought of Richard, and was assailed by such a piercing agony of regret that she gasped and moaned with the force of it.

Numbly she thought, *I didn't know I felt like that. How could I feel like that and not know it?*

She recalled the way he had handled her vase that first time, his fingers running gently over the contours, feeling the curved lines. She remembered how he had made her lunch the day she began work on the dragon, and had waited patiently for her to emerge from what he called her 'trance'. And how he had said softly, 'Well, hello!' when she did. And how he had held her and kissed her, several times, in different ways.

And how he had touched Jane's cheek, saying goodbye. And that he had said, once, when they were fighting, 'I can't leave you like this, hating me.'

She had told him she didn't hate him. But she hadn't known then that she loved him. Now she knew, and maybe it was too late.

In the morning she woke from a fitful doze at dawn, and it was still raining. She got out and stood at the edge of the road, where through a gap in the trees she could see the glacial river, a roaring dragon of a river, hurling boulders of ice and uprooted trees to destruction all along its banks, an eerie, turbulent mist rising from it into the icy air. For a few minutes the sight of it was so awesome and powerful that she almost forgot her predicament, her cramped limbs, her lack of sleep, and even the cold.

At nine o'clock a helicopter flew over and she tried to signal it, but the trees here were quite dense, and she didn't think anyone could have seen her.

Hours later a tractor manned by two brawny Coasters arrived at the other side of the bridge, accompanied by the carver's wife driving a small car. The men, with ropes and planks and a good deal of ingenuity, managed to get Alex across the stream, but the car had to remain where it was. She told them about the state of the ford, and the carver's wife shrugged philosophically, saying, 'Well, I guess Phil can look after himself for a day or two, until the water goes down. I'll stay with friends in town. Anyway, I got some groceries in last weekend, so he won't starve.' And she offered Alex a lift into the township.

The town was coping with disaster. The worst floods in living memory had washed out bridges on both sides of it, and cut the power. Communication with the rest of the country was only maintained by radio-telephone, and there were several hundred tourists stranded, as well as other visitors like Alex. By that evening twenty inches of rain had deluged the area in twenty-four hours. The road to the glacier was washed away, possibly beyond repair. The only way out was by helicopter, and the first passengers to be taken aboard were those who had international flight connections to make.

Eventually Alex was able to get a message out, so that at least Jane could be reassured she was safe. She had no doubt that Charlotte and Albert would care for Jane until she could get home. Meantime she was offered a bed for the night, and some borrowed pyjamas. All she could do was accept them gratefully.

By Saturday it had become apparent that the roads would be closed for days to come. Alex, anxious to get home to Jane, was lucky. Someone squeezed her aboard a helicopter that was heading for Hokitika to pick up supplies for the gangs desperately working in the pouring rain to repair the ruined bridges and roads. From the airport she phoned the Terawitis and asked them to pick her up.

When Richard, his face set in grim lines, flung open the door to the small airport lounge, she stood like stone, wondering if, after the ordeal she had been through, she could be hallucinating.

His eyes went straight to her, and he strode over, picked up the heavy duffle bag at her feet, and snarled, 'What the hell have you got in here?'

'Jade,' she said automatically, wondering why he looked so angry. 'That's what I went for.' She added, 'I was expecting Albert.'

'I volunteered,' he said. 'Come on.'

He took her arm, propelling her through the doorway and out to his car in the car-park.

'I didn't know you were here,' said Alex. 'When did you arrive?'

'Friday. To hear that you were down there at Franz Josef, where they were telling us all hell had broken loose, and nobody knew for sure just *where*. There were bridges washed out in the night, and bits of road that no one had been near for hours. 'They "didn't think" anyone was stranded on them, but they couldn't be sure.'

'I was,' she said, 'but I was all right.'

He opened the car door for her, and slammed it as she got in. Coming round to his seat, he flung the bag in the back seat and turned to face her.

'We didn't know that,' he said. '*I* didn't know that. First my father—now this.' He pulled her into his arms, and with his lips on her hair, then her neck and her cheek, he said harshly, 'I never

want to go through that again. You've got to
marry me, Alex. Give me the right to worry
about you. I've been trying desperately to get
some information, find out where you were, if
you were okay. Everyone wanted to know if I was
a relative before they'd tell me a damned thing, or
get anything done. It's been hell!'

She turned her lips to his, and clung. She felt a
great sigh heave through him as he strained her
close, pushing her head against the leather of seat
back with the force of his kiss.

Then suddenly he held her away, his hands on
her shoulders gripping hard. 'You love me,' he
said, 'Don't tell me you don't. You've got to say
yes.'

She tried to smile, but found she wanted to cry
instead for some odd reason. 'Yes,' she said. 'Oh,
yes!'

Sometimes, afterwards, Alex wondered if the
traumatic experience she had suffered had
affected her more than she realised. Richard gave
her no chance to recant on her acceptance of him.
She hardly had time to break the news to Jane
before he was arranging the ceremony. He
wanted it to take place in Christchurch so that his
parents could be there, and she didn't mind.
When he said they'd find a house in Christchurch,
she smothered a quick feeling of dismay, only
saying, 'Jane isn't used to city life.'

'We can spend the weekends at Akaroa,' he
said. 'She'll like it there. So will you. In fact, we
could live there, if you'd prefer it.'

'No,' she said quickly. 'Your work is in
Christchurch, and especially now that your father
isn't well, you have to be there, don't you?'

'I do, actually.'

'Richard?'

'What is it?'

'You're not—you don't expect me to give up my work, do you?'

He looked astounded. 'Good heavens, no! We'll have to look for a place with a suitable room for your studio.'

'Shifting my equipment won't be easy.'

'No. Well, we won't bother. I'll get you new equipment, the best for our best jade worker.'

Alex protested, 'Richard, no! I can't let you——'

He took her hand. 'I want to—a wedding present if you like, but it's a sound business investment, too. Two birds with one stone. You always thought I was a bit of a shark, didn't you?'

He grinned at her teasingly, and she weakly smiled back, uneasy, but unwilling to spoil his buoyant mood. 'I suppose you're only marrying me to keep my work in the family?'

'Yes. No.' He reached for her and hauled her into his arms, suddenly serious. 'I'm marrying you because I can't imagine life without you any more, because I want you desperately, and for ever.'

She wanted him, too—there was no denying that. They belonged together, they loved each other. Nothing else mattered as much as that. There would be adjustments to make, but they'd work them out. She returned his kiss and lost herself in their mutual desire.

Jane had been remarkably calm about it all, only saying that she liked Richard and she guessed it would be nice to have a sort of father. The news that they would be moving to Christchurch made her thoughtful, but she reacted well to Richard's suggestion that they could have frequent holidays on the Coast, so that she could keep in touch with her old friends, as well as making new ones in Christchurch. 'What will we do with Casanova?' she asked.

'He can go to Akaroa. I could find grazing for him there, if you like,' said Richard. 'Or I can get you another pony to ride.'

Jane chewed her lip. 'We'd be in Christchurch all week?'

'Yes.'

'He'd be lonely. Maybe Mr and Mrs Terawiti would let him stay at their place. He'd be company for Greyboy.'

The fact that the wedding was scheduled for Easter, when the great project of the miner's hut would be finished, helped to reconcile her to the changes in her life.

It was completed in time, and Alex and Richard, along with Shawn's family, were invited to attend the opening ceremony, when Paddy gave Jane the privilege of cutting the ribbon he had tied across the doorway.

After they had admired the rough timber walls and the branch-and-sacking bed, the mining utensils scattered artistically about the hut, and the bright cushion that Jane had made for the single ancient wicker chair, they all repaired to Paddy's house for an impromptu party. It developed into a farewell for Alex and Jane, too, and Alex, joining in a rousing chorus of 'Now Is the Hour' near midnight, felt tears pricking at her eyes as she realised how much she would miss these people.

Paddy echoed her thought when he kissed her goodbye at the door while Richard looked on. 'We'll miss you both,' he said, releasing her, laughing, from the engulfment of his beard and his arms. 'You look after them, Richard,' he added fiercely.

Richard raised his brows. 'I will.'

When Jane had gone off to bed and he was leaving, he said, 'I think Paddy has a yen for you. Strange you two never got together. You seem to have a lot in common.'

'Paddy's a great friend,' she said. 'And he has a lady in Greymouth. She visits him often, and on his day off every Wednesday, he closes the mine and goes to see her.'

They put the house up for sale, Paddy promisng to keep an eye on it. Richard had looked sceptical at the price Alex insisted on asking, but she said firmly, 'With all my equipment in it, it's worth it. If some jade worker doesn't buy it, I'll think about selling that separately and bringing down the price. As it is, I think the price is right.'

'Quite the businesswoman,' he teased.

'I just want to bring something with me when I marry you.'

'Darling, that's nonsense! I'm not looking for a dowry.'

'I know. But you're contributing everything, so far. Don't *smother* me, Richard. I'm not used to being a dependant.'

'Have I been smothering you?' he asked soberly.

'A bit. Anyway, I want to make a contribution, and the house is about all I've got.'

They were married by a simple ceremony in a small church which seemed full of Richard's friends. The whole Terawiti family was there, along with Paddy, and Alex was glad of that, because otherwise she would have looked very much alone in the world except for Jane, who acted as her flowergirl, looking most un-Jane-like in a pale pink dress and white socks bought by Mrs Lewis. Alex, refusing to let anyone help with hers, had bought a new dress, too, pale apricot silk shading at the hem into a deeper tint, and high-heeled shoes to go with it.

Afterwards they all repaired to the Lewis home, skipping a formal reception which neither of them had wanted, and Jane stayed with Richard's parents while he and Alex drove through the dusk to Akaroa.

The little town on Banks Peninsula was reached by the Summit Road, a winding, breathtakingly scenic drive taking in views of the harbour and hills, sometimes on both sides, and of the peninsula itself. Akaroa had been settled by French whalers, and retained the French influence in its old buildngs, and in the names of its quaint, narrow streets. But Richard's house was a modern cottage, built in semi-colonial style to blend in with the atmosphere of the place.

They arrived as it was growing dark, and Richard showed her the small, simply furnished, living room, the bright kitchen and laundry, a spotless bathroom, then a tiny back bedroom and finally the main bedroom with a brass bedhead taking pride of place.

Alex touched the white crocheted bedcover, and pressed on the mattress.

'It's okay,' Richard told her. 'It's pure sponge

rubber, not horsehair. It only looks old-fashioned.'

'Where did you get the cover?' she asked, admiring it.

'My mother made it for me. She helped to furnish the place.'

She was oddly pleased that it had been his mother who added the woman's touch. She wondered if he had ever brought another woman here, but didn't ask.

He had put her bag down with his on the floor, and he came over to drop a kiss on her nape, pushing aside her hair.

'Want coffee?' he asked. 'Or something stronger?'

'I've had enough champagne. Coffee would be nice.'

He made it, and Alex watched and tried to note where everything was kept. As they sat and drank it, looking out the bow window at the darkening harbour until only distant lights and a path of moonlight were visible, she began to feel tense. When Richard spoke, she jumped.

'I'll wash up while you use the bathroom, if you want to. The shower's good, and the water should be hot. The lady who cleans the place turns it on for me Friday nights.'

When, later, he came to her, she was stiff and nervous, and he looked at her with surprise, his arms holding her as she turned her head on the pillow, avoiding his eyes.

'What's the matter?' he asked. His hand smoothed strands of hair away from her face, and his lips caressed her skin.

'I don't know,' she muttered, ashamed. 'I'm sorry.'

'Relax,' he murmured. 'It doesn't matter. We've got all our lives.' He shifted so that she could lie against him, still held in his arms. 'Go to sleep if you want to.'

She sighed against his chest. 'No,' she said stubbornly. 'I want you. I just—just need to unwind a bit, that's all.'

He held her closer, and began to stroke her gently with his hand, soothing her. And after a while she felt her eyelids droop sleepily, her body relax. But as he went on stroking, his hands still exploring lightly but with growing intimacy, something else began to happen to her body. She stirred in his arms, stretched once like a cat, and felt the taut length of his masculinity beside her.

He shifted, bringing her against him, and suddenly she began to respond, her mouth seeking his, her hands touching him in an increasingly exciting exploration of her own.

'Hello!' he said softly, as he had once before in different circumstances, and stifled her answering laughter in his kiss.

CHAPTER TEN

THE new studio was a jade-worker's dream. The house Richard had bought was about ten years old, architect designed and beautifully laid out, with a large lounge and a separate dining room big enough for entertaining.

Alex entertained—business contacts of Richard's and some of his few but long-term friends. The meals she served were always meatless, and no one ever commented, not even Richard. She had bought, mainly with his money and his mother's tactful advice, the kind of clothes she supposed the wife of a successful businessman ought to wear, and they employed a young woman to do most of the housework because Richard said that nothing must interfere with her work. Alex guessed that the standards that had sufficed for her and Jane in their old home with its shabby comfort wouldn't do for Richard, who was used to something rather more classy. The furniture that they chose together seemed too new and too expensive to use without a discomfiting feeling of trespass. And she never became accustomed to having someone else do the breakfast dishes, the vacuuming and the washing, but she would shut herself in the studio after Richard went off to work and Jane to her new school, and try to ignore the sounds of housework being done while she concentrated on turning out the jade jewellery and ornaments that Richard wanted for the shop.

She had not mentioned the heron project to him, and she was not working on it. Sometimes she picked up the piece of white jade and turned it in her hands, brooding, trying vainly to recapture the excitement, the yen for creation. But the familiar exaltation eluded her. The spark had gone.

Never mind, she thought, pushing away her uneasiness. It would come back. It must.

Jane enjoyed the weekends they spent at Akaroa, where she rode a lively little bay pony Richard had given her. But she didn't like the new school, and although she said little, Alex knew she missed Paddy and Shawn, the mine and her old friends, and even Casanova. He might not have been as pretty or as clever as the new pony, but he had been special for Jane. Alex worried about her daughter's new quietness and lack of exuberance, though when she mentioned it to Richard's mother, Mrs Lewis was soothing, pointing out that Jane was growing fast and was probably entering a new phase of her girlhood.

'I think we should have given her more warning,' Alex said once to Richard. 'It's a big adjustment for a child to make so suddenly.'

'It wouldn't have made much difference, surely,' Richard replied. 'The adjustment had to come sooner or later. Kids are very adaptable.'

She stifled an irritated urge to ask 'How would you know?' She knew that she was in danger of taking out her frustration over her dissatisfaction with her work on him, and it was not fair. He couldn't have been more eager for her to carry on with her carving, or more considerate and helpful. There was no way she could blame Richard for her sudden inability to take pleasure in it.

The house on the Coast remained unsold, and Alex took Jane back to it for the school holidays in May, and again for ten days in August. By that time Richard was growing slightly impatient with Alex's refusal to lower the price. He accused her of not wanting to sell at all. Alex inwardly wondered if he might be right, although it was still her intention to do so and to repay some of the money he had spent on the new house and studio in Christchurch. Most of their furniture was still there, and Jane settled into her old routine so easily and happily that Alex experienced pangs of guilt when the time came for them to return to the city and Richard.

She was driving the Mercedes, although the VW, rescued from its stranding in the storm, now shared the garage in Christchurch. Richard had raised his brows teasingly when she insisted on keeping it, had even offered to replace it with a small Japanese car. Alex had flatly refused, and he had given in quite easily, inured now to her occasional displays of stubborn independence.

But he had been quite adamant on her taking the bigger car for the rugged trip over the mountains, in spite of her spirited defence of the Volkswagen which had seldom let her down. Richard had won; he usually did when he was determined on something. Only afterwards, when they had gone to bed and in the darkness he had made to take her in his arms, she had not responded to him.

He said, 'Stop sulking,' and turned her head with his hand, finding her mouth almost roughly, while his hand slid to her breast and caressed it.

Incensed, Alex struggled against him, and he

lifted his head and grabbed at her wrist, pinning it to the pillow.

'I'm not sulking!' she told him icily. 'Let me go.'

'What would you call it, then?' He still retained his hold.

'I'm tired,' she muttered. 'Not in the mood. Call it what you like. Just leave me alone.'

'I call it sulking. You've been "tired" a lot lately, haven't you?'

Alex bit her lip. She had not been tired, really—she had been irritable, tense, vaguely resentful, and she didn't even know why. The first few months of their marriage had been blissful, their lovemaking free and exciting, and she had welcomed it as much as Richard had. But lately her responses had been less ardent, less frequent. There was no reason, unless it was related to her growing discontent with her work, to the near-panic she experienced now and then when she realised that none of the pieces she had fashioned recently were up to her previous standard, in spite of the best equipment that Richard could buy, in spite of the hours she spent on them. They were technically good, but her designs lacked her former flair, and even the lustre on the finished pieces seemed to her inferior.

'You're working too hard,' Richard said. 'Did you always go on until ten at night?'

She hadn't, but tonight she had been trying to get a complicated *pekapeka* design to come out right. In the end she had despaired, and flung down the piece of jade on the bench, leaning on it for a few moments with a strong desire to scream or burst into tears. She had mastered that futile emotion, but the disappointing effect of the day wasted had soured her mood.

She moved her head restlessly, not answering him.

'Alex?' His voice was impatient. 'Alex, look at me.'

The moonlight poured into the room, the shadows making him look almost menacing. But his voice was gentle as he said, 'Tell me what's the matter.'

'I'm not working well,' she admitted. 'I can't get a damned thing to come out right!'

He laughed. 'Artistic temperament, is that all? My God, I thought there was something really wrong!'

'There *is!*' she said fiercely. 'I can't *work!*'

'Darling, don't be silly,' he said, his very patience making her furious. 'Your work is perfect—we're selling it like hot cakes in the shops.'

'Mass production pieces,' she said scornfully. 'Cabuchons set in necklaces and bracelets. And a few fancy curlicues on basically ordinary pieces.'

'They're good.'

'They're unoriginal! I'm not producing *ideas.*'

'You're doing fine,' he assured her. 'Stop worrying, and the ideas will come. You're probably inhibiting yourself by getting tied in knots over it. You've had a few changes in your life lately, that's all, like Jane. Once you settle down, you'll find things will come right.'

He kissed her, coaxing her lips apart, and because she wanted to believe him, wanted to stop the nagging fear that dogged her, she tried to relax and respond. She wound her arms about his neck, and he ran his hands down the smooth skin of them until his fingers touched her breasts. His lips moved warmly in the crook of her elbow, and then followed the path of his hands. But even as her body began to answer the demands of his, her mind remained curiously detached. As though he sensed it, his lovemaking became almost fierce, a demanding, bruising conquest of the senses that finally roused her to a feverish response. She accepted his body, writhing against him almost desperately in an attempt to lose herself in him, in his love, and blot out the nagging worry in her mind. At the height of their passion she drowned for a few brief moments in pleasure, but as Richard drew slowly away, her brain was already retreating from him, wrestling with the problem of the recalcitrant greenstone.

Being back on the West Coast in August, even though the weather was wintry and cold, seemed to revitalise Alex. She drew sketch after sketch for the heron, for new modern designs, for variations of the traditional ones, staying up late, yet waking fresh and ready for more work in the mornings. She had no stone with her, but bought a small piece and began working on a large, complicated pendant at nights after Jane had gone to bed, tired from a day spent at the mine, or with the Terawitis, or, on one blustery, howling day, up the Punakaiki Coast where they travelled to see the Pancake Rocks and their famous blowholes, always more spectacular in stormy weather.

The pendant was not completed when their holiday came to an end, but Alex stowed it in the luggage for finishing later in her new studio.

Jane was largely silent on the way home, and

Alex was unable to draw her out at all. Back at the house, after helping her mother with their bags, she went to her bright modern room with its white-painted furniture and its pretty quilted bedspread, and closed the door.

Alex let her alone for a while, then went and tapped on the panels.

It was a few moments before Jane called, 'Come in.'

She was sitting on the bed, her eyes red and her cheeks flushed, although the tears had been hastily wiped away.

Alex said nothing, just sat down beside her daughter and put her arm about Jane's shoulders, pulling her close.

Jane sniffled a little, and said forlornly, 'I really don't like it here. I want to go home.'

Alex felt her heart sink. 'This is home, now,' she said. 'You've hardly given it much chance, darling. It takes time to make new friends and get used to a new place.'

'It's all right for you,' Jane muttered. 'You've got Richard.'

Carefully, Alex said, 'So have you.'

'It isn't the same. Mum, don't you know where my real father is?'

Alex's breath caught for a moment, and she hesitated before saying, 'Yes, actually I do.'

He had written to her about a year ago, a diffident, apologetic letter, telling her he had married and had a son, and that he was sorry he hadn't been supportive of her when she had needed him, and had asked for a photograph of Jane. He lived in Christchurch.

Jane raised her eyes. 'Do you ever see him?'

'No,' Alex said cautiously. 'We've written to

each other once or twice.'

'Do you think—he'd write to me?'

He had never asked to see or contact his daughter, but Alex knew from the tone of his letter that if he received an invitation to do so he would probably jump at the chance. She had not made the offer, since Jane seemed quite happy as she was. But now it was Jane who was asking for contact.

Alex could veto the idea, hoping that Jane would forget it and that Richard would fill the blank space in her life. She liked Richard, and liking could turn to love. Richard was genuinely fond of Jane, too. He enjoyed her company, and they were surely in the process of knitting themselves into a genuine family.

Alex hadn't given Dennis a thought since her marriage. She had been wrapped up in her new husband, her new life, and in trying to help Jane adjust. He had no claims on them, now, no rights.

But he was Jane's natural father. And he had, belatedly but definitely, expressed an interest in and a concern for his daughter, even to offering Alex financial help which she had unhesitatingly refused.

'Would he?' Jane repeated, her eyes anxious.

Alex said slowly, 'I think so.'

'Could I write to him? Can you give me his address?'

Afterwards Alex realised that she could have offered to post the letter without giving away Dennis's address. Instead, she said, 'As a matter of fact, he lives right here in Christchurch.'

Jane drew in an excited breath. 'Here? Then I could see him—couldn't I?'

'I'm not sure, darling. He has a wife and a—another child. He might not want them to know about—about us. I'm not sure if he's told his wife.'

'Don't married people tell each other everything?'

'Not always. Sometimes it's a bit difficult, if they don't want to hurt each other.'

Jane was silent for a moment. Then she said positively, 'I'd like to see him, though. Will you ask him? Now?'

'*Now?*'

'Can't you ring him up? Ask him to come round?'

Alex frowned, thinking. Dennis had told her where he worked. In fact, it was his business address that he had given her, which made her wonder if in fact he had not told his wife about Jane, or if he was afraid that Alex might embarrass him somehow by turning up at his home unannounced.

'Are you sure that's what you'd like?' she asked.

Jane's answer was positive. 'Yes!'

'I think maybe you should give it some thought.'

'I *have*. I've been thinking about it for simply *ages*!' Jane assured her earnestly. Her pleading eyes, her tightly clenched hands told how important this was to her.

Stunned, Alex echoed, 'Ages? Why didn't you tell me?'

'Well, I thought you might not want to—I mean, you just married Richard, and I s'posed you wouldn't want to be reminded—you know what I mean.'

'I'm not sure I do,' Alex said gently, 'but thank you for thinking of it, anyway.'

'Then you don't mind, really?' Jane asked anxiously. 'I mean, I'd like you to stay with me when—when my father comes, but if you don't want to——'

'I'll stay,' Alex promised. She had decided. Jane wasn't a child to change her mind easily once it was made up. She knew what she wanted, all right. And Alex felt that she had no right to stop her from meeting her father. It seemed important to her. Certainly it was no sudden, idle whim. Probably the desire had been brought on by her uprooting from the home and friends she had always known, but that didn't make it any less valid. Perhaps Jane needed to establish her identity and place herself in the context of her parentage.

She phoned, and found Dennis just as eager as his daughter for the meeting. He hadn't known Alex was married, but laughed and congratulated her without embarrassment before promising to leave work a little early and come round. It all seemed quite natural and normal, and when she told Jane the child merely nodded in a satisfied way and said, 'Good.'

When he came the meeting went off much more easily than Alex had expected. He smiled at her, said, 'You look good, Alex,' and kissed her cheek, before turning to Jane, taking her hands in his and saying quietly, 'Hello, Jane.'

Jane looked at him with frank curiosity, and Alex found herself doing the same. He was older, of course, not the boy she remembered, but a young man with a hairline already tending to recede, and a quick, disarming smile. She remembered the smile, and how it had once affected her, and smiled, too, with slightly saddened amusement at their younger selves.

He held Jane's hands for a few minutes, and said, 'You're like your mum, aren't you?'

Jane wrinkled her nose. 'I guess so. Everyone says I am.'

'You're lucky.'

Jane said mischievously, 'Oh, I don't think I'd mind looking like you.'

The quick smile appeared again. 'Thanks,' he said, and released her hands to pat her briefly on the shoulder.

He asked her about school and friends and hobbies, and she chatted easily to him, but his visit was brief. Just after five he looked at his watch and said he would have to leave. They saw him to the door and watched him walk down the short driveway to the road where he had parked his car.

'He's nice,' said Jane.

'Yes. Jane—he may not be able to see you very often.' Alex was almost sure, now, that Dennis had not told his wife about Jane.

'I don't mind,' Jane said. 'Now I've met him, I know—I mean, I just wanted to know what he was like, I s'pose.'

He had just reached his car when Richard's Mercedes turned in the driveway, and as Dennis drove away, Alex and Jane remained in the doorway waiting for Richard to join them.

'Who was your visitor?' he asked casually as they all went inside.

'My father,' Jane told him.

'What?' Richard stopped walking and stared.

'My father! Mum rang him up and he came round.'

'She *what?*'

Jane blinked at the violence of his tone, the sudden white fury in his face, and her eyes widened apprehensively. Uncertainly, she said, 'Mum rang him up——'

'I heard that!' Richard looked at Alex, his expression ominous. He started to say something, then glanced at Jane, saw the bewildered fright in her face, and clamped his mouth shut, controlling himself.

'I'm sorry, honey,' he said to the child. 'I've had a rough day. I'd like to talk to your mother, if you don't mind.' As Jane looked doubtfully from him to Alex, he managed to smile at her. 'Don't worry, it's all right.'

Jane went off to her own room, and soon from behind the closed door the sound of pop music dimly emerged, played on the portable tape recorder that Richard had given her. He seemed to compensate for what Alex refused to take from him by giving Jane expensive presents.

'I have to make tea,' Alex said into the taut silence in the hall.

'Just a minute.' Richard took her arm and led her to the large, beautifully furnished lounge that she had never felt was really hers. 'What the hell has been going on here?'

The hard suspicion in his voice made her nerves prickle with annoyance. Trying to sound calm, she said, 'Jane wanted to meet her father. I rang him, and he came round. That's all.'

'That's *all?*' he repeated sarcastically. 'He came round, just like that!'

'Yes, actually. What's the matter with you?'

'Oh, nothing, of course! Just, it's a bit disconcerting to come home and find my wife entertaining her ex-lover, that's all—especially when I'd gained the distinct impression that she hadn't seen or heard from him for years!'

'I'm not responsible for your impressions,' Alex said swiftly.

'Aren't you? You didn't even mention that he lived here in Christchurch! It didn't occur to you that I might find that information somewhat—relevant?'

'No, it didn't! Relevant to what?'

'To certain strains in our marriage, perhaps. How often have you been seeing him?'

'I haven't been seeing him at all!' she flashed. 'He's Jane's father, and he has a right to see his daughter if they both want it!'

And Richard, his face coldly angry, said, 'Not in *my* house! Don't you *ever* invite him here again!'

Alex paled, but before she could reply he had turned and left her.

In the morning, after he had gone to work, she went into her studio, taking the half-finished pendant, and began drilling and cutting for the final shaping before working it on the polishing wheel. Grimly, she forced herself to concentrate, not to think about the previous evening, when Richard had been determinedly pleasant to Jane, asking about her holiday, encouraging her to talk and cover the silence between himself and Alex. And the night, when she had lain awake, angry and spoiling for a fight, waiting for Richard to come to bed. But he had not come. She wasn't even sure if he had spent the night in the house, for at last she had gone to sleep, hearing no sound from the living area, and too proud to go and see

if he was still there. When she got up he was fully
dressed and his breakfast things were in the sink.
Somehow that had made her angry all over again.
Her own stomach was churning too much with
tension for her to face food. Richard had said
good morning to her and she scarcely managed a
civil reply, turning her back on him to busy
herself about the kitchen. He had barely glanced
at her again before he left the house.

Jane wandered into the studio and watched her
for a while. Eventually Alex stopped, smiled at
her and said, 'Would you like to go out
somewhere?'

Jane shook her head. 'Do you like it here?' she
asked.

About to say yes, Alex hesitated. She didn't
like it here, she realised. She had tried to, and her
love for Richard and the sympathy and liking she
had for his parents, who needed his support and
help, had held her here. But she didn't like it.
She didn't like the flatness, the orderly city
streets, the calm, civilised atmosphere of the
place. She disliked the clothes she wore, the need
to be polite and gracious to Richard's business
circle, and the way she felt constantly on trial
with his friends, who she was certain were
surprised by his choice and rather contemptuous
of her, in spite of her attempts to adapt to their
way of life. She missed the casual friendliness of
the Coast, its more relaxed life style, the wild
landscape and even the unpredictable weather.
Like Jane, she was homesick. And it was having a
devastating effect on them both.

She knew with certainty, now, that she would
never be able to work here as she had on the
Coast. The atmosphere was wrong, the mystical

stone losing its potency, hiding its potential from her out of its natural environment. She said to Jane, sounding casual, 'There's still some holiday left. Shall we go back—home?'

When Richard found her note that evening, he was curiously unsurprised. Even when he saw that she had taken the VW, not the Mercedes; even when he looked in her studio and found it unusually tidy and clean, and her unworked pieces of greenstone gone, it only confirmed what he had guessed already.

She had written that she and Jane were returning to the Coast 'for a while', and that she would do some work there and send it to the firm as her contract demanded. He knew she wasn't coming back.

CHAPTER ELEVEN

ALEX walked to the window of the studio and held up the *kotuku* to the light. The last careful polishing was finished, and she felt a sense of being drained, mingled with triumphant achievement.

It was perfect, just as she had pictured it in her mind, even better than the drawings she had made before cutting into the stone. The smooth jade caught exactly the white plumage that seemed to reflect the green of lake water, the long, delicate beak was tucked into the breast, the curve of the neck inviting an exploring finger. Feathers were finely etched on the folded wings, and the slender reeds at the base seemed to quiver in an imaginary breeze.

She went back to the bench and carefully packed the *kotuku* in a box with plenty of tissue paper to cushion it. And addressed it to Richard.

She had sent other things in the last few months to the shop, not addressed to him personally. It was almost Christmas, and he would get the parcel just before then.

He had not contacted her since she and Jane had left. She had wondered, at first, what she would say when he demanded an explanation, but he never had. She had expected him daily in the first days and then weeks after the school term started, and Jane, puzzled but pleased, had returned to her old school. Alex had dreaded and yet in a way looked forward to a confrontation. At least on her home ground she felt more confident, less likely to allow him to overrule or persuade her.

After a while, she concluded that he had been relieved to find her gone, that he, too, had realised that they had made a mistake, and decided to call it quits. The thought turned the dull, nagging ache about her heart that she had become accustomed to into an acute, tearing pain, and for days she wondered if she could live with it. She worked long hours at her saws and drills and polishing wheels, and the pain gradually became less and less, though it never entirely left her, and often at night she lay awake, fighting tears and remembering when she and Richard had laid side by side . . .

On Christmas Eve, she was polishing an intricately shaped fish-hook pendant when a familiar engine note made her stiffen and raise her head. She went to the window in time to see Richard emerge from his car, his face grim.

She met him at the door, and they stood for a moment staring at each other, before she silently stepped aside to let him in.

'Jane?' he asked abruptly.

'She's at the mine.'

He didn't go to the lounge, but instead strode into her studio, and she followed him.

He looked about and then turned to face her. 'How is she?' he asked.

'Fine. Very happy to be back.'

'Is that why you left?'

Alex hesitated. A mother couldn't be blamed for thinking of her child above all else. But that was an excuse. 'Not—entirely,' she admitted. 'I wasn't happy, either.'

'Obviously. You didn't think it worth explaining to me?'

'I couldn't. It was difficult to put into words. You would have thought me very—silly.'

'Maybe I would. I still think I was entitled to an explanation, though.'

'You've taken a long time to ask for one.'

For the first time Richard showed anger. 'What was I supposed to do? Come running after you, begging to be told why you were leaving me?'

'No.'

'No.' He looked at her with smouldering temper in his eyes. 'Why did you send me the heron?'

'I—thought you'd like it,' she said huskily.

'A Christmas present. It was a message, too, wasn't it? No card, no note, just the most exquisite piece of work you've ever done, sent to me. I did get the point, Alex, but you could have told me before you left.'

'I wasn't certain then,' she said huskily. 'I thought—maybe it was something I'd just lost for good, that I wouldn't be able to work here, either. And I did tell you I couldn't work anywhere else. I even talked about the problem not long before I left. You laughed at me.'

'Laughed?' He stared, and she reminded him defensively, 'You laughed and said it was just artistic temperament.'

'I laughed from sheer relief,' he said abruptly. 'I'd been thinking all kinds of things—that you regretted having married me, that you didn't love me after all. As it turns out, I was right, but at the time, when you said it was your work that was worrying you, I thought, Thank God, it's only that!'

'*Only!*'

'Oh, God! I'm not devaluing your talent, or trying to suggest it's unimportant. I know it's important to you—more important than I am.'

'That's not true,' she said swiftly.

His face hard, he said, 'Yes, it's true. It's a ruling passion. The one thing in life you can't do without. Nothing else can satisfy you, fulfil you. Marriage and jade carving apparently don't go together. And you chose the jade. I'm not blaming you—It hurts like hell, but I'm trying to understand. You can't help the way you are. I'm sorry if marrying me killed your talent. Still, it seems that leaving me had the desired effect of bringing it to life again. The *kotuku* has all your old flair.'

He couldn't keep the bitterness from his voice. Distressed, she begged, 'Richard, please stop! It wasn't your fault. At least, I suppose in a roundabout way it was. You married me, and took me to Christchurch, to the plains. But it wasn't being married to you that affected me, not that in itself. It was having to live in Christchurch, to live anywhere away from the Coast. I can't be myself there. I can't——'

'Express yourself in your work,' he finished for her.

'Yes,' she said, 'I suppose that's what it is. It isn't that I chose the jade above you, please believe that.'

'Trying to soothe my ego, Alex? That's not like you.'

With a flash of temper, she said, 'No, I am not! I'm trying to explain. The jade—the work—it's not something I can choose or not choose. It's a part of me, and without it I'd be less than myself.

Can you begin to understand that? I would be crippled without my work, just as much as if I had lost an arm or a leg, or an eye. Would you ask me to prove I love you by cutting off my arm?'

'*Would* you?' His brows rose with fierce, ironical humour.

She considered it quite seriously for a moment. 'I would do it to save you from death or maiming,' she answered slowly. 'Not just to satisfy you that I cared for you. Because that, if you asked it of me, would be perverted, immoral.'

'I never asked you to give up your work.'

'I know! I know you didn't! You asked me to be your wife. And I wanted to be. But it can't work, because I don't fit into your world, Richard, your life. You were right.'

'I never said that,' he objected. 'I never even thought it.'

'Yes, you did, not in so many words, but it was how you felt. That last day, you said to me, "Not in *my* house." I hadn't realised it so clearly before then, but it *was* your house. I never felt at home in it. Your house, your life, not mine. I have to live my own life, Richard. I'm sorry. Perhaps because I've been alone so long, I can't suddenly become an extension of you.'

'I've not expected you to,' he said. 'I don't believe in that kind of domination.'

'Not consciously, perhaps. But that's what it amounted to, in the end.'

'In *your* mind! Not in mine.'

'In *fact*,' she said. 'It's just the way things are. I should never have accepted you, never imagined that I could settle into being your wife. We knew how different our backgrounds, or life styles, were. I'm not cut out to be Mrs Richard

Lewis. I was a failure at that, and when I found I was failing at my carving, too, it was—devastating. I had to salvage something.'

'You were not a failure,' he said, 'at anything.'

'I was. I hated dressing up for dinner parties and social functions. I was nervous and inadequate, hostessing for you. Your friends found me—peculiar.'

'That's utter rubbish! The only real friends I have were fascinated by you—and a little bit frightened.'

'*Frightened?*'

'That's right,' he said, to her astonishment. 'Especially the women. They were afraid of boring you, of being themselves with you, because of your talent, your ability, even your strength of character. They were overawed by you.'

'That's crazy!'

'Maybe. It's the truth.'

Alex shook her head disbelievingly.

Impatiently, Richard said, 'All right, don't believe me. It isn't important.'

He moved closer to her, his eyes intent. He took her face in his hands and said, 'You might have been feeling out of your element, but the catalyst was seeing Jane's father, wasn't it? I know I reacted badly at the time. I hadn't any idea that you and Jane had been in touch with him. It seemed you'd been keeping a whole part of your lives from me. A man who'd been that close to you—and you had been growing farther and farther away from me.'

'It wasn't like that. It was the first time Jane had seen him—the first time I'd spoken to him since she was born. I tried to tell you that we hadn't been meeting as you seemed to think.'

'Was that true?'

'Of course it was. He had written to me months before, asking about Jane, and I replied, that's all. That day, she was upset about coming back from the Coast, and I discovered she'd been thinking about her father, wondering about him. She wanted to see him, and I thought she should, she had that right. I think in a way I hoped it would help her to settle in Christchurch. But she didn't specially want to keep up the contact, anyway. She satisfied her desire to see him, and that seemed to be sufficient, for the present.'

Richard's hands had moved to her shoulders, but his eyes still held hers intently. 'So you hadn't actually seen him for some time?'

'Not for years. When I did see him in the street, after Jane was born, he avoided me. Then he left the district the following year. He was only a boy, then. He's matured since, begun to cope with responsibilities. He seemed quite a different person.'

'Do *you* want to see him again? Did you find you still felt something for him that you couldn't feel for me?'

'Oh, no!' she said, involuntarily raising a hand to place it over one of his. 'No! I asked him round for her sake, and all I felt was a sort of sad blankness.'

'Is that how you feel about me, now?'

'I love you,' she said simply. 'I know it sounds incredible, when I can't—won't live with you, share your life. But it's true.'

'And I love you,' he said soberly. 'I can't leave my parents and the business—well, not for a long time, you know that.'

'Would you?'

'To be with you, yes. But I can't just shelve all my obligations.'

'I never thought you would,' she said. 'In any case, it's not expected of men, to follow their wives. Not men like you, anyway.'

'I told you before,' he said, 'you've got a conventional streak a mile wide. You never thought to look for alternatives, did you? You just cut and run.'

'I didn't think I had any right to ask you to disrupt your life, or to choose between me and your parents, your own way of life.'

Roughly, he said, 'You didn't even ask me to discuss the problem! We're married, Alex. Don't you think you owed me something in the way of explaining how you felt?'

'I'm sorry. I just didn't see that you could possibly understand. And I suppose I didn't think I could explain it adequately, either. I didn't know what had happened to me. Just that I'd lost something vital to me—inspiration, perhaps, the creative spark, or the atmosphere necessary to produce it. I don't know. Even now, I can't really express what I felt. At the time, I was completely unable to even try. I needed to come back here to sort myself out. Believe me, when I left it was with the hope that I could come back. Only, the longer I stayed here, the more I realised that this is where I belong, where my work belongs. I couldn't have carved the *kotuku* anywhere else. It was when I had done that that I knew for certain I could never go back. The Coast, the greenstone—they belong to each other. It was a sort of betrayal, to leave it. But I didn't expect that to mean much to you, even if I managed to put what I felt into some sort of words.'

'Well, thanks for your confidence!' Richard

dropped his hands, walked away a couple of paces with angry restlessness, then turned again to face her. 'All right, I admit I don't fully understand, even now. But I'm willing to try. Even without understanding, I'm willing to compromise, try and work things out, somehow. I want to stay married to you, even if we can't always be together. I thought you'd stopped loving me, but the heron gave me a different message. I was sure you wouldn't have sent it if you didn't still feel something for me—something deeper than liking, or remorse or pity.'

'I couldn't put it into words,' she said. 'I hoped that when you saw the *kotuku* you'd begin to understand.'

He came back to her, put his hands on her waist and looked at her face, his mouth grim, his eyes searching hers. 'Perhaps I am—beginning to,' he said. 'Promise me you won't send me away.'

'I won't do that, Richard. I want you to stay for ever. But I know you can't.'

He kissed her, gently at first and then deeply, with growing passion. Alex kissed him back, with an unreserved passion of her own, deliberately inciting him with subtle movements of her body until she felt him shudder with desire. 'When will Jane be home?' he whispered, his lips on her throat.

'Not for ages,' Alex murmured dreamily, her fingers trailing along his shoulder under his jacket.

'Good.'

He picked her up and carried her through to the bedroom. 'You fought me last time I suggested this,' he grinned as he joined her on the bed.

'I'm not fighting now.' She slid her arms about him, and met his kiss with parted lips.

'I don't know why you thought I wanted you all dressed up like a dog's dinner,' he said, sliding up her tee-shirt. 'I knew that first day that you weren't wearing a bra. I find it very sexy.'

A slow warmth was growing inside her. Her hands tangled in his hair, her breath quickening, she said, 'Richard, can we really work it out? You in Christchurch, and me here. It won't be a conventional marriage.'

'I don't want a conventional marriage. It was the unconventional about you that attracted me, I think, in the first place.'

'Supposing I get pregnant again?'

'We'll work it out,' he said, raising his head to look at her. 'I promise. Without jeopardising your jade work. Would you mind—having my baby?'

'I wouldn't mind,' she said. 'I wouldn't mind at all.'

He smiled down at her. 'Is it possible?'

'Very possible.'

'Barefoot and pregnant sounds rather suitable for you.'

She closed her fist and, laughing, hit softly at his shoulder. 'Didn't I say once, scratch a middle class liberal, and you'll find a male chauvinist?'

'Didn't you say once that you loved me?'

'I do.'

'Then nothing else matters. Stop talking, woman, and kiss me.'

She stopped talking. For quite a long time.

'Jane will be home soon.' She lay against his bare chest, listening to the steady beating of his heart.

His fingers trailed down her spine. 'Will

she be pleased to see me?'

'Yes. She's missed you, but she's happier on the Coast, too.'

'Do you know, I think I was even more upset about Jane preferring her natural father than I was about you having him in the house,' he confessed.

Alex sat up. 'You love Jane, don't you?'

'Yes. I missed her, too.'

'She may want to see her father again when she's older. I wouldn't stop her, Richard,' Alex warned.

He saw the determination in her face, and her fear that he would oppose the idea. With an effort he swallowed his jealousy, conceding her right as Jane's mother to make that decision.

He said, 'You're right, of course. I'll have to try to accept that. By then I hope we'll have established a relationship, become a family.'

'So do I.' She smoothed the faint frown between his brows, and kissed him lightly. 'Don't look like that. Jane's fond of you.'

'It wasn't Jane I was thinking of.'

She hesitated, starting to draw away, but he caught her wrist in a hard grip. 'It won't be just Jane seeing him, will it?'

'Probably not. You have nothing to worry about, Richard, I promise.'

His eyes searched hers, then he relaxed. 'I'm sorry. You know, when I first saw him—when Jane told me who he was—I had nightmare visions of you with him, of—oh, I don't know. You going off with him and Jane, leaving me. And you did leave me.'

'Not for him. Not for any man. There'll never be another man for me, now.'

'Nor another woman for me. We still have so much to learn about each other, so much to explore. I want to know you, I always wanted to know more about you, all your thoughts, your feelings, your beliefs, not just this, your beautiful body.' His eyes and hands caressed her as he spoke.

Alex held herself away from him a little. 'I want to know you, too. But it won't be easy, with a part-time marriage.'

'Not a part-time marriage, a full-time one lived in two different places. I'll come to you often. Will you come to me sometimes?'

'Yes, of course, when I can.'

'How about starting now? It's Christmas. My parents would like to have you and Jane there for Christmas dinner with us.'

'Oh, yes! A family Christmas.'

'Will you stay till the New Year?'

'Yes, please. I'd like to start a new year with you. It would be—appropriate, don't you think?'

'Very.' Richard pulled her down to kiss her. 'I don't know how I'll part with you when the time comes,' he murmured. 'I'll probably be here on the doorstep the very next weekend.'

'I'll be waiting.'

'Always?'

'Always,' she promised.

Richard gave a long, satisfied sigh, and turned her in his arms until she lay beneath him again.

'Jane,' she murmured as he lowered his mouth again to hers.

'Mm, I know. She's coming home.' Reluctantly he released her, and lay watching lazily as she gathered up her clothes.

'You look smug,' she accused him, laughing.

'I feel smug. How do you feel?'

She stopped laughing and said soberly, 'Wonderful. It's been so—oh, Richard, I know it was I who left you, but there've been times when I thought I'd die if you didn't come.'

For a moment he looked grim again. 'You never called me.'

'No. I wanted to, but it wouldn't have been fair.'

'God! Don't you know how miserable I've been without you?' he burst out violently.

'I thought you were probably relieved, in a way. I'm such an unsuitable wife for a man like you.'

He suddenly reached out and pulled her down again on the bed, shaking her. 'That is *nonsense*! Don't ever say anything like that—don't even *think* anything like that, again. You are clever and beautiful and honest, and all that any man could possibly ask for. How I got you, I don't know, but I'll never let you go again, separations or no. So make up your mind to that. Physically we may have to be apart far too much, but in every other way we'll be so close you'll be with me every second of the day, and every night. I'm going to be as much a part of you as your jade. You might as well know that.'

'You already are. Didn't you know? All the time I've been working, since I left you, you've been a part of me—a painful part, until now.'

'And now?'

'It won't be painful any longer. But you're still part of me. And I don't have to fight that any more.'

'Never fight it, Alex. Never again.'

She smiled, reaching up her hand to trail it

over his face until he caught it and pressed his lips to her fingers. 'No more fighting,' she promised huskily. 'Anyway, you always win.'

He remembered the first time he had seen her, and how she had challenged him. Looking for a fight, he had thought, and mentally he had determined to accept the challenge, and to win.

Now he looked down at her flushed face and the tender laughter in her eyes, and he grinned back at her and said, 'Yes, I do.'

NEW ZEALAND'S KAURI TREE

New Zealand, the setting of Daphne Clair's Presents, is known for its high-quality jade. A somewhat lesser-known natural resource, but one just as valuable in its own way, is kauri wood.

The kauri (rhymes with dowry), a tree indigenous to New Zealand and other islands of the South Pacific, is similar to the giant redwood of California. A kind of pine, it is considered one of the world's truly great trees. Few experiences compare with entering a kauri forest. The trees' silvery gray or reddish gray trunks soar more than a hundred feet into the sky, where they are crowned by evergreen branches that softly filter the sunlight into the forest below. Some are more than twenty feet around, and they can live for centuries. In New Zealand's Waipoua Forest stands an enormous kauri tree the Maoris have called "Tane Mahuta"; it is said to have reached maturity more than 2,000 years ago!

When settlers first arrived in New Zealand, kauri forests covered the countryside. In those days, the trees were used to build houses – one tree supplies enough wood to build an entire house. As well, kauri wood was used for the tall masts of great sailing ships. The wood's beautiful wavy grain, free from knots because the trees have few branches, has today made kauri wood most valued for making furniture.

Because kauri trees were once felled with no thought to conservation, and because they grow very slowly, the trees are quite rare today. Most are now protected in national forests, but each year a limited amount is cut and used by craftsmen to create beautiful pieces of fine furniture.

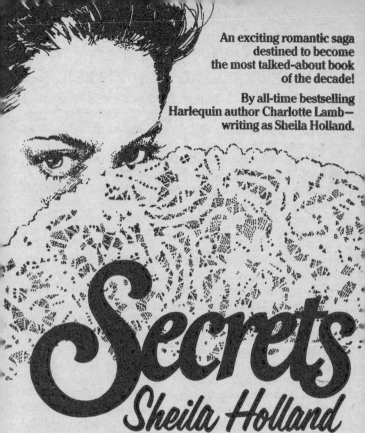

THE GOLDEN CAGE

The first Harlequin American Romance Premier Edition by bestselling author ANDREA DAVIDSON

Harlequin American Romance Premier Editions is an exciting new program of longer–384 pages!–romances. By our most popular **Harlequin American Romance** authors, these contemporary love stories have superb plots and true-to-life characters–trademarks of **Harlequin American Romance**.

The Golden Cage, set in modern-day Chicago, is the exciting and passionate romance about the very real dilemma of true love versus materialism, a beautifully written story that vividly portrays the contrast between the life-styles of the run-down West Side and the elegant North Shore.

Watch for *The Golden Cage* at your favorite bookstore in April, or send your name, address and zip or postal code, along with a check or money order for $3.70 (includes 75¢ for postage and handling) payable to Harlequin Reader Service, to: Harlequin Reader Service

In the U.S.
Box 52040
Phoenix, AZ 85072-2040

In Canada
649 Ontario Street
Stratford, Ontario N5A 6W2

GC-2

"No. You're not a fool, Mr. Lewis."

His narrowed eyes were fixed on her face. "Thanks. I'd like to be able to return the compliment."

Flushing with anger, she said, "Don't worry. I know exactly what you think of me. You look down your middle-class nose at me and my clothes and my life-style."

"You don't have any idea what I think of you." He looked at her with exasperation before continuing. "You *are* a fool, Alex Cameron."

Unexpectedly Richard's hand shot out to grasp her shoulders and pull her up against him. He bent swiftly to kiss her mouth, the pressure of his lips brief and hard against the startled softness of hers.

"And the name is Richard," he said as he released her abruptly and slammed himself into his car.

Books by Daphne Clair

These books may be available at your local bookseller.

For a free catalog listing all titles currently available,
send your name and address to:

Harlequin Reader Service
P.O. Box 52040, Phoenix, AZ 85072-2040
Canadian address: Stratford, Ontario N5A 6W2